REAWAKENING

Sydney Campbell

ISBN: 978-1-7774505-0-2

Cover design by abu-chan
Editing by Megan Records

For my ray of sunshine.

Other books by Sydney Campbell:

Allie Styles Romance Series:
Temptation (Book 1)
Deception (Book 2)
Reckonings (Book 3)
Beginnings (Book 4)

Courtyard Tales of Contemporary Romance
Reawakening
Redemption
Reckless

CHAPTER ONE

Louisa

I blamed the bird.

I was standing at the sink, washing my dishes from breakfast when the cardinal first appeared outside my window. Of course, I noticed him. I lived on my own, was always alone, and had come to relish the little bits of company I had.

He was dashing. Bright red, and when the sunlight caught him, it looked as if his feathers were made of pure fire. I was completely distracted and dropped the plate I was drying. I jumped back as it shattered into pieces, scattering across the floor.

At least it's Saturday. I'd have taken it as a bad omen if it had been a workday. Broken plate, another broken marriage. After four years, my work as a divorce lawyer was starting to wear me down. Watching families fall apart on a daily basis would do that to you.

But nothing could have put a damper on that particular Saturday. For the first time in fifteen years, I'd be seeing Ian Mackenzie. My best friend through high school and college, we'd parted ways when I got married. He went off to become a sculptor and travel the globe, while I'd stayed put, gotten married, divorced, and ended up in family law hell. He'd been living the life while I'd been learning to be alone.

Ian was coming to town to pack up his late father's apartment. Mr. Mackenzie had passed away suddenly, and as the only child and surviving family member, it was up to Ian to settle his affairs. He was due to arrive at around eleven. I checked the clock on the wall. It was a quarter to.

I bent down to pick up the pieces of ceramic. As I tossed them in the trash, I managed a nasty gash on my right index finger. I yelped as I watched the blood flow and got up to run it under cold water. When the stars stopped swirling behind my eyes, I found a dishtowel, wrapped up my hand, and went in search of bandages. I was sure there were some somewhere. Maybe the bird had been an omen.

The bell rang as I was midway up the stairs. I paused, feeling a flutter of excitement. Ian. I turned and raced down the stairs, slowing myself to a halt as I got to the door. I didn't want to appear desperate.

There he stood. Handsome as always, perhaps even more so due to the subtle lines around his eyes and mouth. They gave him that sexy, rugged look. He had dark curly hair, peppered with grey now, that fell just past his ears. He grinned when he saw me, his smile reaching his dark eyes, which widened and lit up when I opened the door. He was in great shape; that was apparent even through his leather jacket. Plainly put, he was drop-dead gorgeous. Just like I remembered from high school.

"Lou!" he cried, sweeping me into a giant bear hug.

I couldn't stop the smile that broke out. I held his shoulders as he swung me around and planted a kiss on my cheek.

"Mac," I said, inadvertently reverting to his high school nickname.

He smiled as he set me back down.

"How you been, Lou?"

"Why don't you come inside and I'll tell you?"

I opened the door wider and he followed me

inside. For the first time in the five years since I'd moved into the house, I cursed myself for not having done the necessary renovations. I was living in the past. I'd inherited the house from my mother and the furniture had belonged to her mother. It was 2020 and I was surrounded by florals and brocade. The drapes didn't even open anymore, the mechanism long broken.

It had never bothered me before. I had grown blind to it all, living in my little bubble. But now, seeing it through his eyes, it was painful. I cringed to think what was going through his mind.

"Shit," he said. "Exactly like I remember it."

He turned around, taking it all in. Then he shifted his gaze to me, studying my face.

"I mean, exactly. Everything okay, Lou?"

"Everything is fine, Mac."

He nodded and showed himself into the kitchen. He rifled through the cabinets until he found himself a glass, then opened the fridge in search of a drink. He pulled out a container of orange juice and poured himself a glass. Even though we hadn't seen each other in fifteen years, it was completely natural. He pretty much lived in this house while we were growing up. But now, the kitchen seemed tiny and he seemed so...huge. Almost as an afterthought, he looked at me.

"Want some?"

"It's okay. I just ate."

He nodded again and downed his juice.

"I'm so sorry about your dad," I said.

"Yeah. It really sucks that he was on his own. I was due to visit in a couple of weeks."

"How often did you visit him?"

"As often as I could. At least four or five times a year."

"And you never called before this?"

He looked at me for a long time.

"I only found out recently about the divorce."

"And the idea of my marriage is what stopped you from calling?"

"Let's just say death makes you reevaluate things."

This had gotten awfully serious, awfully fast.

Ian and I had been close at one time. Extremely close. Always platonic, though. He was like a brother to me. One I got along with. He was that guy in high school that everyone loved. He was sweet but had an edge. He didn't judge people, no matter their social status. And he was popular. I was not. We only met because I was assigned to be his peer tutor in English and history. Over the course of the year, we became friends, and it stuck. Until I got married.

"So what have you been up to?" I asked, trying to lighten the mood.

"Shows, mainly. I've had openings all across Europe, and quite frankly, I'm glad that's done with. Have you heard about this virus? Man, it's scary as hell."

"I know. I've been following it very carefully. In case you don't remember—"

"You were the world's biggest hypochondriac," he finished for me. "Still?"

"Still."

"Well, in any case, I'm hoping to find somewhere to stay put for a while. I haven't created anything in months, and it's killing me. I need to set up a studio and get to work."

"Where?"

"Haven't decided. All my shit is in storage here for the moment. And now with this virus…"

"Well, in any case, I'm happy to see you. And you're welcome to crash here tonight if you need a place to stay."

His eyes lit up once again, that grin reaching his ears.

"Really, Lou? That would be great. I'd love the chance to crack open a bottle of wine and catch up."

I grinned back. It was so good to see him.

My life had been filled with a lot of anger and bitterness, and let's face it, loneliness. I tried to stay upbeat through it all, but my life was getting me down. Seeing Ian again drove it all home. I had strayed very far from my path and was starting to have regrets. It would be nice to have him around.

"Let me go make up the bed in the spare room, and then we'll hit the grocery store. It's been a long time since I cooked for you."

"Oh my god, Lou. Let me do something for you."

"Just rest."

I got up from my seat at the table and went upstairs.

CHAPTER TWO

Ian

I was nervous as fuck. There's no other way to describe it. I watched as Lou went up the stairs to prep the room for me and all I could think about were the fifteen lost years between us. I'd been such an ass.

From the moment our high school principal led her into the classroom and told me Louisa was going to tutor me, I was smitten. She was cute as hell in her purple sweater and pink-rimmed glasses. And her smile. Christ, that smile.

I didn't even notice her eyes until the second or third time we got together. They were always hidden behind those glasses. I loved watching her push them up her nose, grimacing slightly as she did so. It was charming as fuck. Though at 16, I was probably just having hot librarian fantasies. Then one day she showed up, and poof, no glasses. Contacts, she'd said. Her eyes were magnificent. Wide and bright blue, and so crazy curious.

I made a point of getting to know her. To do that, I had to pretend to be really slow in history. I couldn't bring myself to fake it in English. I wanted to impress her too badly for that. But I quickly learned that the harder it was for me to remember dates and the details of all those wars, the more sessions we needed.

I could've just asked her out, but I didn't have the guts. She was nowhere in the same league as my crowd when it came to money and popularity. And even though none of that mattered to me, I was still a 16-year-old kid who felt the need to belong and was scared to rock the boat. In the back of my mind, I always thought I'd have college to tell her how I felt, but she met that bastard so damn quick. My vision went black just thinking about how that dickhead treated her. I couldn't stick around and watch. So I split.

And then there I was, sitting in her damn kitchen and waiting for her to make up the spare room for me. It was every teenage dream come true—a sleepover at Lou's house. But I'd lost my chance long ago. We were strictly in the friend zone. And as ridiculous as it felt to even think those words at forty years old, I knew they were true. But that didn't mean I couldn't have her in my life. And judging by the look of her house, maybe she could use me in hers.

I heard her come back down the stairs and looked up as she walked through the kitchen door. It was damn hard trying to keep it casual. After all this time, and all the women I'd been with, no one made my heart race like Louisa Taylor.

True, she'd put on a few years, but so had I. She was still hot as ever, but now it looked like she just didn't give a shit, which brought its own brand of sexiness. Her hair was longer, had some grey, and she'd put on a few pounds. But it suited her. I liked curves. She'd always been too skinny in high school, and it only got worse in college. Now she looked like a woman.

She held up her hand, which for the first time I noticed was wrapped in a rag or something. In her other hand she held a box of bandages.

"Found some bandages."

"Christ. What happened?"

"Oh, nothing. A plate broke just before you came in. I cut myself cleaning it up."

She unwrapped the rag and put her finger in her mouth, sucking slowly. I was instantly hard. I shifted in my seat, looking away. I tried to disguise my groan with a cough, but I'm not a hundred percent sure I fooled her.

By the time I turned back to face her, she had wrapped up her finger and was reaching for a glass from the cabinet. I got a good look at her ass, and my cock twitched. I shifted again, completely unprepared for this turn of events. I was a forty-year-old man. Spontaneous erections weren't exactly my thing.

She turned and flashed me a smile.

"So? What do you want for dinner?"

You.

"How about steak? You still eat meat or you go all vegan like those other activists?"

Louisa snorted.

"I'm not sure you can call a divorce attorney an activist."

I sat up straight. What the fuck was she talking about?

"Divorce attorney? What the fuck, Louisa? Last time we spoke, you were saving the world."

"Yeah, well now I'm saving women who were screwed over by their bastard husbands."

This was not cool. I had never heard a cynical note in Louisa's voice *ever*. A new surge of rage boiled through my veins at the thought of what that asshole might have done to her to put it there. I took a deep breath.

"This is the career you want?"

Her face broke, and for a moment I saw the old Lou. She shook her head sadly.

"No. It was the career I thought I wanted. After he left, I wanted to protect other women like me. But all I do is watch families fall apart. I miss my old work."

She sat down opposite me, and I had to restrain myself from reaching out to take her hands. Instead, I leaned over and ruffled her hair. It got a smile.

"So? Go back."

"It's not so easy, Mac."

Mac. Every woman I'd ever known called me Mac. Every woman I'd fucked. And there were a lot. But this was Lou. I wanted her to call me by my name. She bit her lip and I completely lost my train of thought. How many nights had I jerked off to the memory of exactly that expression on her face? I reached under the table for a quick adjustment, rapidly losing executive functioning.

"I'm sure you can figure it out. Maybe I can help while I'm here. I'm around for a couple of weeks, at least. Let's spend some time together."

I held my breath. *Too much, too soon?*

"Spending time with you sounds lovely. Let's put a pin in the other thing for now. Tell you what. Why don't you take a nap? I'm sure you had a long flight. I'll go get the stuff for dinner. We'll catch up then."

She leaned over and kissed my cheek. Then she grabbed her keys off the counter and left the room. I heard the door close behind her and finally exhaled.

I got up and went upstairs, poking around in the rooms until I found mine. I walked in and stripped off my jeans and shirt. Climbing into bed, I resolved to nap. I knew I needed it, but it was no use. I had a raging hard-on that wasn't going anywhere. I shoved my hand down my boxer briefs and stroked absently, bringing to mind that woman I fucked in Paris, right after my last show. She'd had these huge, incredible tits and she'd let me come all over them. But no. My mind kept drifting back to Louisa. Her ass, her face as she sucked on her finger. I wrapped my hand around my shaft, pulling harder, pumping as I thought about that mouth wrapped around my cock. I slid upwards, over the head, closing my eyes and groaning as I imagined her on her knees, looking up at me with those blue eyes. One more pump and I came all over my stomach, waiting for my breathing to return to normal before reaching over for a tissue.

Louisa.

CHAPTER THREE
Louisa

I finished searing the steaks on the range and was sliding the cast-iron pan into the oven to finish them off when I heard Ian moving around upstairs. It was funny how he was always Ian in my head, but whenever I opened my mouth to say his name, Mac came out. Everyone called him Mac. Who was I to claim a different name?

I busied myself dressing the salad, but looked up to smile at him when he walked into the kitchen. He was freshly showered, still-damp hair dripping on the shoulders of his white T-shirt. His faded jeans hugged his hips then fell to his ankles. He was barefoot.

I remembered the very first time I walked into that classroom and saw him sitting there.

My heart practically leapt out of my chest. But as soon as my brain caught up, I realized I'd never have a chance with someone like Ian, and I quashed those feelings down quick. I was glad I did, otherwise our friendship would never have blossomed. And even though we'd lost fifteen years, I could already tell he was back in my life to stay.

He nodded at me and got to work collecting plates and cutlery to set the table.

"Did you have a good nap?" I asked.

"I did. Thanks. And thanks so much for doing all this. Let me treat you to dinner tomorrow."

"I'd love that."

We smiled at each other and I turned to pull the steaks out of the oven. He uncorked the wine and poured us each a glass. By the time we sat down to eat, it felt like we'd been doing this routine every night for our entire lives.

"Lou," he said. "I'm really sorry the marriage didn't work out."

So much for small talk.

"No, you're not. You never liked him."

"No, I'm not. I never liked him."

Ian was silent for a moment.

"But I am sorry he hurt you. That you were hurt. I never wanted that."

I nodded. It was never any secret that Ian

hated my ex. I always knew in the back of my mind that was the reason we drifted. I lost my way with a lot of my friends while I was with him. Okay. All my friends. Emotional manipulation was his specialty. It wouldn't have served him well if I'd had outside opinions to consult. Which was pretty much how I found myself lost and alone when he left.

"I know," I murmured. I tried to shift focus a little. "What about you? Never married?"

He laughed, that great throaty, sexy laugh he had.

"No. No marriage for me. I'm never in one place long enough."

"It's not lonely?"

"Um...No. I find company. A warm bed in every port, you could say."

I rolled my eyes. Typical Ian. I refilled our wine glasses, then lifted mine for a drink.

"What about you?" he asked. "You dating?"

I almost spit out my wine.

"Mac. Do I look like I'm dating?"

"You look great, Lou."

"Liar." I took another sip. "No, I'm not dating. I haven't dated since my marriage exploded. At first, I was too angry, too bitter. Now I'm just too fucking tired."

"What about sex? You're telling me you

haven't had sex in six years?"

I snorted.

"Longer than that. The marriage was dead before we called it."

"Lou."

I shrugged.

"I've got a drawer full of toys and a ready supply of batteries. What can I tell you?"

Ian blushed slightly, which was incredibly endearing. I couldn't recall ever having embarrassed him before. Mind you, I couldn't have imagined ever saying something like that to him before. I guess it's true what they say about women in their forties—no fucks left to give.

"You never long for human touch?" he asked, obviously still perplexed. "You don't even have a pet."

"Look, Mac. When you've been alone as long as I have, you adjust. Maybe I'll date again one day. I don't know. I'm fine. Really."

We spent the rest of the meal talking about his art. He'd become so successful in such a short time, but he was still the same old Ian. He was down-to-earth, funny, and kind. So kind he even laughed at my jokes. I pulled out a chocolate cake I had picked up at a local bakery, and put on some water for tea. He was looking tired, but I didn't want the night to end yet. I wasn't ready to let him go. It was wonderful to just talk to him again.

It occurred to me that maybe things were starting to turn around in my life. After so many years of solitude, I met a new neighbour the other day. Allie had just moved into the courtyard with her husband, Matt, a few months ago. After five minutes of conversation, I realized I'd made a friend. She was bright, witty, and had a definite edge to her that I enjoyed. Like she was keeping some kind of secret. She'd quickly become a magnet in the courtyard, attracting everyone, and with good reason.

For me to have made two friends within a week was unprecedented. I looked at Ian, smiled, and resolved to savour every moment.

CHAPTER FOUR

Ian

Dinner was fantastic. I'd forgotten what a kick-ass cook Lou was. I'd spent the better half of a decade eating in the top restaurants in the world, but that meal beat them all. I started to panic when I saw her pull out the dessert and put up the tea. I was not ready to let her go to bed.

As soon as she finished eating, I got up.

"Why don't you go put your feet up in the living room?" I suggested. "I'll clean up in here and join you in a minute."

Had to be proactive.

She smiled up at me as I leaned in to take her plate. I could smell the faint musk of her perfume mixed with the red wine in her glass. It was intoxicating. And after that comment about the sex toys. I straightened abruptly and turned my back to her as my dick betrayed me once again. I didn't turn around again until I heard her get up and leave the room. I let out a sigh and cleared the plates. I then searched frantically through the kitchen, desperate to find another bottle of wine. Finding one, I uncorked it, picked up our glasses, and joined her in the living room.

She was curled up on the couch, looking adorable. She had a blanket thrown over her and was peering over the back of the couch out the window. I took a breath and went to sit beside her, handing her a glass of wine. She looked up at me and smiled, taking it from my hand. Her fingers brushed mine and I pulled away, settling into the couch.

"Dinner was amazing, Lou. Thanks."

She smiled, saying nothing.

"I've been thinking about what you said earlier," I started. "I really think you should start dating again. I hate to think of you alone here. Any guy would be lucky to have you."

She snorted and looked me in the eye.

"Like you would have given me the time of day in high school?"

I was silent. If only she knew.

"Come on, admit it. You'd have never dated me." Clearly, she wasn't giving up.

"I didn't think you'd have anything to do with me," I said quietly and picked up my wine.

She just rolled her eyes and changed the subject.

"I've been thinking too," she said. "Why don't you stay with me a few days until you sort things out? What was your plan? To stay at a hotel? At your dad's? I could use the company."

She didn't have to ask me twice, but I didn't want to appear too eager, either.

"You sure?" I asked. "I've got a reservation downtown."

"Cancel it. You're staying here."

I smiled. We were both silent as we drank. She didn't seem any more eager than I was to call it a night. I asked her what it was like living in her childhood home, which led to a whole discussion about all her neighbours. It sounded like a pretty interesting lot. She was all about this one chick, Allie. At least I knew she had people if needed.

"Listen, Lou, I wasn't going to ask, but—"

"Anything, Mac. What is it?"

"The funeral is tomorrow. I was wondering if—"

"Of course I'll come. It's not even a question."

With that, she threw off her blanket and stood up, putting her empty glass on the table. She threw me a smile and then stretched as she yawned. I watched the thin cotton of her shirt stretch over her tits and closed my eyes. *Fuck.*

"It's past one," she said. "I am going to sleep. What time do we need to leave?"

"Around 10:00 a.m.," I said, clearing my throat.

She nodded.

"Okay, I'll see you in the morning."

With that, she turned and went upstairs. I watched her go and then took my time finishing my wine before heading up to bed for another round of furious jerking off.

CHAPTER FIVE

Louisa

For the first time in a long time the next morning, I woke before the alarm. And I woke up with a smile on my face. Then I remembered we had a funeral to go to and the smile vanished. But even though the morning was tinged with sadness, I couldn't shake that happy feeling that came with knowing Ian was back in my life. I'd missed him more than I'd realized.

I got out of bed and grabbed my robe, wrapping myself up before opening the door and heading to the bathroom. The door was shut, and I heard the shower running, then it shut off. I stood there for a moment, paralyzed. Should I go back to my room and wait? Or was he done? I was so unused to sharing living space, I'd forgotten what the etiquette was.

Before I had a chance to sort it out, though, Ian walked out of the bathroom with nothing but a white towel wrapped around his waist. His hair was dripping wet, and beads of water were still cascading down his chest. He saw me standing there and his eyes widened momentarily. Then he grinned, reached out to tousle my hair, and brushed past me.

"Hope I left you some hot water, Lou," he called playfully.

I was frozen to the spot. I could still feel every inch of skin where his body had brushed up against mine as he walked past. It was like fire dancing. It was a wholly unfamiliar sensation, and it stirred a feeling in me that I hadn't felt in a long, long time. What the hell? This was *Ian*. I blushed furiously. Maybe he was right. Maybe it had been too long since a man touched me. If just slight contact sent my heart racing with *Ian*, of all people, then maybe I did have an itch to scratch. I made a mental note to bring up the subject of dating again. Maybe he had a friend or two in town he could set me up with.

I continued to the bathroom and took my shower, setting it considerably colder than I normally liked it. Hell, I'd bragged to Ian about my toys, but the truth was, I hadn't even masturbated in over six months. The drive just wasn't there. I had honestly thought that at forty, that part of my life was over. Maybe I was wrong.

I finished up in the bathroom and returned to my bedroom to dress. I chose a black, fitted wool dress that I hadn't worn since before my divorce. Mainly because I could never do up the zipper by myself. I was just doing the clasp on a string of pearls when I caught Ian's reflection in the mirror as he passed by my door.

"Hey, Mac," I called. "Can you come in here and help me out for a minute?"

He walked into my bedroom and all of a sudden he seemed huge. Once again, his presence filled the room. He was dressed in a dark suit, open shirt collar, no tie. He hadn't shaved, and what looked like two days' worth of stubble lined his cheeks. His hair curled down past his ears. I was suddenly having trouble breathing, and I was *very* aware that the back of my dress was completely undone, revealing the top of my lace panties and the back of its matching bra. Ian was just staring at me.

"I just need a zip," I said, casually pointing a finger over my shoulder like I did this every day with gorgeous men. Then I turned my back to him and bit my lip to avoid saying anything else.

I closed my eyes as I felt his warm fingers trailing along my back, following the path of the zipper. Then I opened them again, remembering I was standing in front of a mirror and he could easily see my face. If he was looking. Which he was not. His gaze was fixed on my back. I held my breath. When he got to the top, he carefully did the little hook-and-eye clasp and then patted me on the back. He cleared his throat as he stepped away.

"I'll meet you downstairs," he said and walked out the door.

My heart was thumping. And I was *wet*.

Lou, get a hold of yourself. This was my best friend I was lusting after, on the day of his father's funeral. It was just wrong. The whole situation was wrong. I wondered if I'd made a mistake inviting him to stay. I glanced towards the famous drawer of sex toys and quickly realized I had nowhere near enough time. Or privacy.

For the first time in recent memory, I was horny.

CHAPTER SIX

Ian

The funeral was rough. In the end, I was glad I worked up the guts to ask Lou to come. My dad was a great guy, and the turnout was good, but there was no one there I felt close to. Lou was beyond gracious and invited everyone back to her house afterward. She called the neighbourhood deli from the car and by the time we got back to her house, the food had arrived. We just finished setting up when the first guest came through the door.

I spent most of the afternoon off to the side, just watching Lou as she moved through the crowd, making sure everyone had what they needed. She was perfect. It was as if this was an event she'd been planning for weeks. I marveled to myself that this woman had chosen to spend her days and nights alone. But as much as I appreciated everything she had already done for me, I just wanted everyone gone so I could be alone with her. The later it got, the more unlikely that seemed.

When the last guest finally left, Lou turned to me with a soft look in her eye.

"You must be exhausted," she said.

"Yeah, kind of. Also a little wound up."

She nodded and put her hand on my arm.

"I'm going to go up to bed. I know it's early, but it was an emotional day."

She gave a little laugh.

"I guess I don't have to tell you that," she added.

Then, as if on a sudden whim, she reached up and hugged me. Without thinking about it, I wrapped my arms around her. Who knew if I'd get another chance? Our entire bodies were touching, but all I felt were her tits pressed against my chest. I tried to think of my dead father. She got up on her tiptoes and whispered in my ear.

"You smell just the same."

Sorry, Pops. All thoughts of my father flew from my head, rapidly replaced by images of my face between Louisa's legs. I shook my head and pushed her away abruptly.

"I didn't know I had a smell," I offered

feebly.

She gave me a lazy smile, her eyes in a far-off place.

"Oh, yes. And it's still there."

With that, she turned and went up to bed.

*

I slept late the next morning and it felt terrific. I hadn't realized how the pressure had built over the last few days, and with the stress of the funeral behind me, it was like a giant weight lifted off my shoulders. It was past eleven by the time I rolled out of bed. Lou had long gone off to work, so I took care of all my shit and then tried to figure out what the hell I was going to do with myself.

I'd be spending the majority of time cleaning out my father's place, but I needed a plan. I needed to get back to work. I needed to do something with my hands. I looked around Lou's house and once again shook my head at the state of disrepair. I got up, grabbed a pen and pad off the coffee table, and did a slow tour of the house. An hour later, I had a complete list of shit that needed to be fixed. By the time she got home from court, I'd been to the hardware store and was fixing the curtains in the living room.

"Mac! What are you doing?" she asked.

"Just a few little things here and there. Don't worry about it."

"You really don't have to do this. It's fine. I have plans to get it all taken care of."

"Uh-huh." *My ass, she did.*

She took off her coat and hung it in the hallway. She was wearing some kind of skirt and jacket thing. She looked very serious. It was not a side of her I was used to. She flashed me a smile.

"I'm just going to go up and change. I'll be right back."

She took off upstairs and I climbed down from my ladder and went to the kitchen. I'd started dinner earlier—a pasta bolognese—and I wanted to make sure everything was on schedule. She walked in a few minutes later wearing sweats and a T-shirt, her hair all up on her head in some kind of knot. I just wanted to sweep her up in my arms. I turned back to the stove.

"You were serious about treating me to dinner," she observed.

"Of course," I said, turning to her with a smile.

I held out the spoon for her to taste the sauce. She looked a little skeptical, but leaned in and licked the spoon, her delicate little tongue flicking out for a second. I swallowed my groan. Her eyes widened in surprise.

"Mac, that's delicious."

I smiled and turned back to test the pasta. I knew the sauce was good. It was the only thing I knew how to make. It was how I impressed all the women I fucked. But tonight, I just wanted to nourish this woman. Spoil her rotten. I wanted to fix up her house, her career, her life. I wanted her to be happy.

She reached up to get some plates and set the table. By the time I sat down with the pasta, she had already poured the wine. She lifted her glass and looked at me over the rim.

"I've been thinking," she said, almost shyly. "Maybe you were right."

"Oh, yeah? About what?"

"About getting out there again. Opening myself up. Dating."

I swear to Christ, my heart stopped. I put down my fork and swallowed. *Don't even go there, asshole. Just listen to what the woman has to say.* My dick was listening, I could tell you that much.

"Oh, yeah?" I said, trying to act casual.

"Yeah."

She put down her glass and looked me straight in the eye. I held her gaze.

"Maybe you've got some friends in town you

can introduce me to?"

I felt like I'd been fucking sucker-punched. I had to fight to keep from vomiting. I gave her a quick smile and took a swig of my wine.

"Yeah. Sure. I'm sure I know a few guys."

I finished my dinner in silence. There wasn't much to say after that.

CHAPTER SEVEN
Louisa

Ian had only been with me a week and already the house looked completely different. I had started spending evenings shopping for furniture online. With some plaster repair and a new paint job, the living and dining rooms were looking sharp and the centuries-old furniture was just a slap in the face at this point.

Work had been rough the past few days and it was nice to have someone to come home to. Especially someone like Ian, who gave incredible foot rubs. We'd gotten into a routine of him waiting for me with dinner and a bottle of wine, and then we'd enjoy a nice evening on the couch talking, reminiscing, and tossing around ideas for the future—both our futures.

He still hadn't decided where to live, and I was starting to form a crazy idea in my head.

One evening, I was coming up the walk and I heard Allie call my name. I turned towards her house and found her standing on the front porch, her dog Loki beside her.

"Allie! I'm sorry I haven't gotten in touch. I've just been busy with—"

"Ian, yes I know," she laughed. "Come in, have a cup of tea with me."

I glanced towards my own front door, for once anxious to return home, but decided to take Allie up on her offer. It was nice to have a friend in the courtyard—finally—and I figured I could probably use a sounding board. I was starting to form some pretty irrational thoughts in my head.

I walked over to her house and followed her inside. She let Loki off the leash and he bounded into the dining room to his water bowl. I loved Allie and Matt's house. It was bright and airy—the complete opposite of my own. Allie took off her coat and went straight to the kitchen to put on the water. I followed her in and leaned up against the counter to wait with her.

"So? Spill already! I saw him coming and going and Louisa, he's gorgeous."

"He is, isn't he?"

"Louisa!"

"There's nothing going on, Allie. But I've got to say, having a man in the house again is doing strange things to me."

Allie laughed. She had a great laugh. I smiled.

"I'm serious. I'm walking around with a low-level throbbing in my pants all the time."

"And you say it's platonic."

"It is! Trust me, Ian and I are just friends. He would never even consider me in that way. But I've been without a man long enough that just the sight of him in a towel or the smell of him after his shower is enough to get me going. God, Allie. I'm dying."

"You need a release."

"I do. I've asked him to set me up with a friend."

"You did? Louisa! That's amazing. And?"

"Nothing yet. I'll nudge him tonight."

I picked up my tea, testing it to see if it was still too hot. It was perfect. We talked about the house and the work they'd been doing, and I filled her in on Ian and the repairs he'd been tackling. At least an hour passed before I heard the key turn in the front door. I jumped as Loki raced down the stairs and passed us in the kitchen on her way to the front door. I heard barks and Matt's laughter as she greeted him.

Moments later he appeared in the kitchen, giving me a little nod but heading straight to Allie like there was nothing else in the universe.

I'd watched them move in and was struck by the obvious connection between them. You could practically see the sparks fly when they touched. And they touched often. He had recently returned from a month away, but whether he was gone for five minutes or five weeks, it was always the same greeting—a mad, hungry kiss. It made my knees weak to see it. I couldn't imagine what it did to Allie.

I coughed, trying to be discreet. Matt pulled away from Allie and grinned sheepishly at me.

"Sorry, Lou. How you doing? Who's that hunk you got over there?"

I laughed.

"Just an old friend, Matt. Sorry to disappoint you."

"I am disappointed," he said. "I was hoping maybe you were getting a little action."

"Matthew!" Allie cried.

He silenced her with another kiss. That was my cue. I put my cup down and picked up my briefcase.

"Thanks for the tea, Allie. It was great to catch up. Let's do it again soon."

Allie broke away from Matt and looked over

at me, smiling her infectious smile. I couldn't help but return it.

"You don't have to go," she said.

"I do. Ian will have dinner waiting."

"Oooh," Matt said. "Just friends, huh?"

I rolled my eyes at both of them and grabbed my coat.

"Thanks for the gift, Allie. I'll put it to good use."

I smiled at her and she smiled back. Matt gave her a puzzled look and she elbowed him in the side. He pulled her hair and kissed her neck. They were really too much. Almost made my heart ache.

*

We were sitting in the living room, relaxing after a delicious dinner of Thai takeout. Turned out that pasta bolognese was the only dish Ian knew how to cook, so every night since he'd been ordering in. Suited me fine, so long as I wasn't the one worrying about it. I knew money wasn't an issue for him. He'd passed the "starving" stage of artist many years ago.

We'd already knocked back a bottle and a half of wine when I remembered Allie's gift from earlier. I reached for my purse and fished around.

"What are you doing?" Ian asked.

"Just looking for something," I mumbled. Then I looked up at him. "Do you remember that time in high school—I think it was eleventh grade—when Steve Lebofsky gave you that joint and we smoked it behind the school?"

Ian burst out laughing.

"I do. That was a great day. Best math class ever. It made sense for the first time."

I laughed as I found what I was looking for. I pulled a freshly rolled joint out of my bag and held it up for Ian to see. His eyes widened.

"Get out. Where'd you get that?"

"Allie. I stopped in for tea on the way home. You wanna—?"

"Damn straight, I wanna. Lou! In a million years, I'd never have guessed."

"Well I don't, really, I just thought it would be fun with you. You know, for old time's sake."

I was feeling the effects of the booze and was starting to wonder if throwing weed in the mix was such a good idea. But it was too late to back down now. Besides, if anything went wrong, Ian would take care of it. And if he couldn't, Allie and Matt were just a few steps away.

I handed him the joint while I got up to look

for matches and something to use as an ashtray. By the time I settled back down beside him, he'd already lit it up with a lighter he had in his pocket. I raised an eyebrow.

"I'm a Boy Scout. Always prepared."

I laughed and swung my feet up into his lap as I lay back against the side of the couch. He passed me the joint and I took a few tokes, small ones as it had been almost twenty years since the last time I got high. I told Ian about my day, which had been horrid, and he once again went on some rant about how I had to reevaluate my career choices. As the weed set in, I lost track of what he was saying.

"Hey, Ian. Did you ever get me that date?"

I hadn't meant for it to come out so abruptly. He was actually in the middle of a sentence. But the wine and the weed were doing nothing to alleviate that low-level throbbing I'd complained to Allie about, and suddenly the idea of a man between my legs seemed like a really good idea.

"As a matter of fact, I did," Ian said. "He wants to take you out next Friday. The thirteenth, I think. You good with that?"

"Blind date on Friday the thirteenth? That some kind of joke?"

"Never knew you to be superstitious."

I rolled my eyes at him.

"Who is he? How do you know him?"

"His name is Joel. We went to art school together. He divorced a few years ago. Stand-up guy. I think you'll get along."

As he spoke, Ian picked up one of my feet in his big hands and started to knead my soles. It felt amazing, and I melted into the couch as he spoke. He looked over at me, amused, but continued what he was doing.

"He wants to take you to dinner. That work?"

"Yeah. Thank you, Ian. I didn't expect anything so quickly."

"I wasn't taking any chances. If I can leave you knowing you're on a good path, I'll feel much better about things."

The pot had hit me full force by this time. I had remembered fits of giggles in high school, but this time I just felt really mellow and really in tune with my body. I closed my eyes and could feel tiny little sparks going off where Ian touched me. He was now working my heel, digging his fist into it, erasing all the tension from my day.

"God, that feels so good," I moaned.

Ian cleared his throat and shifted my legs a little in his lap. He sat up a little straighter, trying to get comfortable. Apparently unable to, he picked up my feet and shifted a little further down the couch.

"Where you going?" I asked. "That felt amazing. You didn't even finish the other foot."

"Just a cramp in my hand. It'll be fine. I'll get you tomorrow, don't worry."

He flashed me a smile and kneaded his knuckles into the palm of his other hand. I got on all fours and crawled over to him, taking his hand in my own and taking over the massage.

"That's not necessary, Lou. It's fine."

He was breathing funny and not looking me in the eye. It must have been the pot. I had no idea how long it had been since the last time he smoked, but he wasn't very giggly either. Somehow, the air got very heavy in the room, and I was aware of every sound, every movement. I turned to survey the room, then turned slowly back towards him, looking him in the eye.

"I think I'm high."

He pulled his hand away from mine and tousled my hair.

"I think that's a safe bet," he said. "Maybe you should get to bed."

"Tell me more about my date, Mac. What's he like? He cute?"

"He's a great guy, Lou. I promise. I would never set you up with an asshole, you know that. And if he misbehaves, let me know. I'll deal with him."

"Maybe I want him to misbehave."

I was stunned that the words had come out of my mouth. It was so unlike anything I'd ever say. I think Ian was stunned too because his jaw just dropped.

"It's been a long time, Mac. More than six years. You've convinced me I'm ready. So I'm ready. But now all of a sudden I'm terrified because what if I don't even remember how to kiss?"

He smiled at me, soft and sweet. He leaned in close, just inches from my face, and spoke quietly.

"Lou. You don't ever forget how to kiss."

"How do you know?" I breathed, my heart racing from how close he was to me.

I could smell his cologne, the same one he'd worn forever. That smell that brought me back to our younger years, when we had no idea of the paths that lay before us. I just had to close my eyes, breathe him in, and I'd be back there, the whole world stretched out before me at my feet. A different world.

"I know," he said, startling me out of my reverie. "It's easy. Look."

And with that, Ian leaned forward the last two inches and kissed me. Softly, almost chastely, but on the mouth and for a bit longer than I expected. A rush went through me, leaving me completely breathless and paralyzed. The low-level throbbing between my legs cranked up a few notches to burning need. In the twenty-five years we'd known each other, Ian had never kissed me before. Ever. As my shock dissolved, the realization set in that he was a phenomenal kisser. And there wasn't even any tongue involved. Just as I was starting to lose reason, he pulled away and smiled.

"See? Just like that."

And then he got up and went upstairs.

CHAPTER EIGHT

Ian

I lay on the bed, staring up at the ceiling. *What the fuck did I just do?* I hadn't smoked in over six months, and the wine combined with the weed, and then the way she just crawled over to me. Christ.

I had to apologize. I knew I had to apologize. Otherwise shit would just be awkward. I heard her come up the stairs and close the bathroom door. I stared at the ceiling some more as if some magic fucking ceiling fairy would tell me how to deal with this. I ran through possible explanations as I heard her leave the bathroom and go back to her room. It took me a few more minutes to screw up the courage, but I finally got up and pulled on a pair of sweats. I'd knock on her door, tell her it was the booze and the weed and hoped she'd forgive me. I could be charming when I needed to be. I was sure I could pull this off.

I stepped out of my room and walked the few steps to her door. It was slightly ajar, the winter weather warping the wood—I hadn't yet gotten around to planing it yet. I was about to knock when I heard a click and the unmistakable sound of a vibrator switching on. A sound I knew well. *Shit*.

I should've turned and gone back, but I was worried about creaking floors and how embarrassed she'd be if she knew I was standing there. I was just about to attempt an escape anyway when I heard a soft moan escape her lips and my semi turned into a full-on hard-on.

Ian, you asshole, you will not look. You will not look.

"Oh, oh, yes..."

I bit my lip and grabbed my crotch, trying desperately to readjust. I leaned up against the wall and against my goddamn will shoved my hand down my pants. It was too much, listening to her on the other side of that door. My cock demanded attention.

"Oh, yes. Oh, Ian..."

What the fuck?

I pulled my hand out of my pants and

turned towards the door. There was a sliver of space where the hallway light shone into her room. I could faintly make her out, on her back, naked, one hand on her tit and the other holding the vibrator between her legs. As I watched, she slowly slid it in and out, writhing beneath it, her fingers pulling at her nipple. I suppressed a groan as she pulled the vibrator out and used the tip to tease her clit. My hand escaped back into my pants as her hips bucked up as if they were beckoning me. I pried my eyes away and leaned back up against the door, pumping frantically as I listened to her moan and call my name. As soon as I heard her go over, I came into my hand, panting and sweating up against the wall. *Fuck.*

I heard the bed creak and made my way back to my room. No way was I getting caught spying on her. Dammit. I had not meant to spy on her. But Jesus Christ, she called my name. What did that mean? *It meant nothing.* It meant she hadn't had sex in over six years and I kissed her. That's all. I got into bed, shut out the light, and went the fuck to sleep.

*

I was already at the table drinking coffee when Lou came down the next morning. She was dressed, hair up, and looked like she was stressed out.

"What's the matter?" I asked.

She looked over at me, distracted, then smiled as if noticing me for the first time.

"Nothing. Just a big case today. Not looking forward to it."

"We'll do something fun tonight. Take your mind off things."

She flashed me an even bigger smile.

"That would be amazing, Mac. I'd love that."

She leaned over and kissed me on the cheek. Then she was out the door.

CHAPTER NINE

Louisa

When I'm in court, one hundred percent of my attention is on my client. That day, I was defending a young woman of 26 whose abusive about-to-be ex-husband was trying to sue for support. He claimed that, by agreement, she had been the breadwinner in the family and he was entitled to the lifestyle he'd become accustomed to. No way that asshole was getting away with it. Even though my client had been too frightened to report him during the marriage, I had amassed enough evidence and sworn affidavits to prove how he'd treated her over the course of their four tumultuous years together.

But as soon as I stepped out of that courtroom, my brain was flooded with images of Ian kissing me. I had to brace myself against the courthouse wall as a rush of heat spread through my body, gathering between my legs. I remembered the previous night, the vibrator skimming over my clitoris, imagining it was Ian teasing me. I got goosebumps just thinking about it. It was insane. Ian. My oldest and dearest friend. I was convinced that it was because he was a man and living in my house, but whatever the reason, the truth was undeniable—I was having inappropriately lustful thoughts.

I went back to the office for the afternoon, working on a few other cases I had going. My earlier victory had bolstered me, but I knew Ian had been right. It was time for me to get out of divorce law. I was forty, for Christ's sake. I wasn't *old*. I still had so many work years ahead of me, and it was ridiculous to spend them doing a job out of spite, rather than focusing my energy on something I loved. I started mentally preparing for how I'd make the transition, and before I knew it, five o'clock had rolled around and I was heading out the door.

Over dinner that night, I watched Ian as he moved around the kitchen getting dinner sorted out. He always refused to let me help him, which was silly because he was already doing so much around the house. It had never looked better and it was almost surreal to have faucets that ran and cabinets that closed. But I knew he was itching to get back to his art. I watched as his large hands opened the containers, dishing the food into bowls and onto plates. I closed my eyes and pictured those hands running over my breasts. My eyes snapped open and I shook my head. *Stop it, Louisa.*

"So, Ian, I was thinking...About Joel," I said.

His back was to me, but I saw him stiffen ever so slightly.

"Yeah? What about him?"

"Any idea where he plans to take me?"

It was as if all the air went out of his body. He just kind of *deflated.* His head dropped and he shook it slowly.

"No, sorry, Lou. No idea. Want me to find out?"

"No, that's okay. I was just curious. I don't even know what to wear."

He turned to me and smiled.

"You look great in anything, Lou. You know that. You're smoking hot."

I laughed, maybe a little nervously. I prayed he didn't notice my nipples harden at that comment. It really had been too long. I was pretty sure I was safe though because his eyes never left mine. My pulse was pounding in my ears, and it was a few seconds before he broke contact and turned back to the food. It was only then I realized I'd been holding my breath.

I shook my head, trying to clear it of absolute fucking nonsense. Having this much testosterone around was messing with my brain.

"So, Mac, have you thought about your plans at all?"

He paused on his way to the table, a serving dish in each hand.

"Why? You want me out?"

I looked at him, surprised.

"No, nothing like that. Don't be ridiculous. I just know you wanted to get back to work. You seemed kind of anxious about it."

He'd finished packing up his father's stuff and was almost done settling the estate. I knew it was only a matter of time before he would be gone. It wasn't that I wanted him out, I just didn't want to be blindsided.

"Yeah, well, I've got a few more things to finish up here. If that's okay."

"Mac. Of course, it's okay. Stay as long as you want. I love having you here."

I turned my attention to my food and we ate

in a semi-awkward silence. I felt like I'd done something wrong but for the life of me I couldn't figure out what. For the first time since he'd come to stay, Ian didn't join me in the living room after we ate. He mumbled something about meeting a friend and left the house. Six years I'd lived in that house by myself, but never before had I felt so alone.

CHAPTER TEN

Ian

I'd fucked up. And good. Not only was she keen to go on her date with Joel, but she was also practically begging me to move out. I never should have kissed her. Dammit.

I pulled my jacket closer, hoping the neighbourhood dive was still around. It was. I walked in, went straight to the bar, and ordered a scotch. I needed a plan. I needed to find a way to stick around and keep Lou in my life. It had only been a couple of weeks but already I dreaded the thought of losing her again. It had probably been a mistake, going to see her in the first place. Any hope I had of winning her over was gone now, thanks to my pathetic lack of control.

I finished my drink and ordered another,

taking a moment to look around. There was a gorgeous blond sitting at the end of the bar. She caught my eye and smiled, then turned away. My head wasn't in the game, but my dick twitched. The bar was playing eighties music, and Soft Cell came on singing about tainted love. I finished the second drink and told the bartender to make the third a double.

When I looked up again, she was right there beside me. I smiled.

"Hey," I said, trying my damnedest to sound noncommittal.

"Hi. You here alone?"

"Isn't that supposed to be my line?" I asked.

She laughed a cute little airy laugh.

"But you didn't ask me."

"What are you drinking?"

She smiled and settled onto the stool next to mine. She looked me up and down, then glanced at my drink.

"I'll have a scotch."

I raised my eyebrow. No girly shit for this one. I ordered her a drink and she starting making small talk. I didn't know what the fuck I was doing. I knew I wasn't going home with her, but I hadn't yet figured out how to tell her that. I just hadn't had the heart to turn her away. I got into a lot of trouble that way.

We sat there drinking and flirting until the

bar closed down and kicked us out. She looked at me expectantly, and I realized I was going to have to do something. I opened my mouth and before I knew what hit me, she grabbed my collar and kissed me. I'm not dead. I kissed her back. She pulled away and looked up at me with her hooded blue eyes, giving me that look. I knew that look. I sighed.

"Listen, it was great hanging out. Really. But I've got to head home. Early day tomorrow."

She looked at me, dumbstruck.

"Are you fucking kidding me?"

"I am not. I'm sorry."

She looked at me for a long time, then shook her head slowly.

"Un-fucking-believable."

She turned on her heel and walked away. *Crap.* As soon as she was gone I put my hand on the back of a nearby bench to support myself. I was fucking wasted. If she had kissed me again, things might have gone a very different way.

*

By the time I stumbled into the house, it was past 3:30 a.m. I bumped into the entryway table and swore under my breath, not wanting to wake Lou. Everything was dancing around before me. I put my hand on the wall to guide me, not wanting a repeat performance of my crash entry.

I went to the kitchen for some water and hopefully a bottle of Tylenol. I fumbled around in the cabinets. Nothing had changed in this fucking house in 25 years, but suddenly I couldn't find a thing. After I had my water, and no pills, I turned to head upstairs. The light coming from the living room caught my attention and I walked over to check it out.

Lou was curled up on the couch, hands tucked under her head, fast asleep. She looked peaceful, and I stood there and stared at her for good long time. Still so goddamn cute. Sleep erased the worry from her face, and with her eyes shut I didn't have to see the loneliness that had settled there. I shook the cobwebs from my head, walked over to the couch, and covered her with a blanket. Then I grabbed another blanket, the pillows off the love seat, and got comfortable on the floor.

CHAPTER ELEVEN

Louisa

I sat on the sofa, cross-legged, watching Ian sleep. He was sprawled out on his back, fully clothed, with a blanket tossed across his torso. The light was streaming in through the window, thanks to the newly-repaired curtains. I'd replaced them with cream linen ones, and already it made a world of difference lightening up the room. I was just waiting for the new furniture to arrive.

As the ray of sunshine moved across the floor, I waited. I contemplated getting up to make tea, but I didn't want to miss the moment he woke up. I needed to witness his moment of shame. Just the thought made me smile. After I don't know how much time, he finally stirred. When the sun hit him, he threw an arm over his face and grunted. I saw one eye open, then the other. Then he sat straight up.

"Shit!"

I laughed.

"You okay?"

He looked at me as if seeing me for the first time. He rubbed his eyes, then looked down at his clothes. He looked around, momentarily confused.

"You must have had a good time last night," I said. "Tell me, this friend. Is she anyone I know?"

He stared at me blankly.

"She?"

I gestured vaguely to his face.

"You're covered in lipstick. And the smell of perfume coming off you is stronger than the booze."

And for the second time in our friendship, Ian blushed.

"Nothing happened," he said quietly.

"Uh-huh," I said, getting up.

I tiptoed my way around him on the floor and went to the kitchen. I pulled out the eggs, milk, and cheese and got some water going. As I prepared omelets and toast for us, he eventually stumbled into the kitchen and took a seat at the table.

"You want me to go, Lou?" he asked.

"Go where, Mac?"

"I don't know. Just leave."

I turned around, surprised.

"No. What makes you say that?"

He shrugged.

"I dunno. Yesterday you asked how long I was staying."

I turned off the stove and slid the omelet onto a plate, bringing it to the table along with a couple of other plates and some cutlery. I sat down next to him.

"I just know you want to get back to work, that's all. Stay as long as you want. Really. I like having you here."

He smiled but still looked unsure. I got up and reached into one of the upper cabinets, pulling down a bottle of Tylenol.

"Fuck, that's where you keep them," he said.

"What?"

"Nothing."

He took the pills from me gratefully and swallowed them with a swig of water. Then he continued eating in silence. I gathered he was suffering. It was Saturday, so at least he had the day to recover. I had planned on running some errands but quietly decided to stay in and hang out with him. If he was thinking of taking off, I wanted to get in as much time as I could.

After breakfast, he went up to shower and take a nap. I tidied up and then wandered into the living room to plan out, for the hundredth time, how I'd arrange the new furniture. My gaze drifted over to the dining room, beyond which lay a closed-in sun porch my parents had built about 15 years ago. It was huge, almost the length of the house, and heated for our cold Montreal winters. I was using it for storage, which was a shame as it got so much light. I walked over to the glass doors, which were located on the sidewall of the dining room, and stared at the boxes piled up. The room contained a lifetime of my parents' memories.

I turned and walked to the basement door, opening it and walking carefully down the old steps. I pulled the chain to light the single hanging bulb and surveyed the room. Semi-finished, it was pretty empty. I glanced back upstairs and thoughts started spinning in my head. Nice thoughts. Dangerous thoughts.

The truth was, I wanted to keep Ian with me as long as I could. I knew we were only friends, but having him around just made me feel better about myself. I felt connected to someone. As much as I'd convinced myself I was fine on my own, his presence had shown me I wanted more. And more was impossible with Ian. He was a world-renowned artist. I was a small-time divorce lawyer. I was nowhere in his universe. But I also knew he loved me, and I could tell he wanted to see me on a different path. Maybe he'd stick around a while for that, at least until I found someone more on my…level. Maybe even this Joel guy.

Who are you kidding, Lou? I mean, really. He was a world-class artist. Why would he care how my life turned out? I shook my head, tossing the thoughts from my head. I'd actually been thinking of proposing turning the sunroom into a studio for him. He would've laughed at me. Well, maybe not to my face, but he certainly would've laughed about it.

Maybe with the mystery woman.

CHAPTER TWELVE

Ian

The week sped by. It took me two days to recover from that hangover, and then once Monday rolled around, things seemed to just pick up speed. I watched as Lou grew increasingly nervous about her upcoming dinner date. Every night she came down in a different dress, asking my opinion. She took off to Allie's house at least once or twice a day, "for tea," she said. Yeah. I knew women a little better than that.

It was killing me, watching her getting so worked up. I knew exactly what she was thinking—she'd go out with this guy, and even if it didn't work out, at least she'd get laid. That's the part that killed me. That it would be fucking Joel and not me. What had I been thinking, agreeing to set her up?

But even more than Lou, I was getting really stressed about the virus. Confirmed cases in the city, talks about social distancing. What did that even mean? All I knew was I was glad to be with Lou and not alone in some hotel. I had a feeling lockdown was coming soon. I'd been watching Italy, and I knew it was only a matter of time.

By Thursday, it was crystal clear that the time had come. Schools were shutting down, businesses closing their doors. I dreaded Lou's return from work. I knew she wouldn't be going in the next day, but I also knew her date was pretty much dead in the water.

I made the pasta bolognese. Things had been okay between us during the week, but still a little tense. I never got the chance to explain the lipstick. There was no logical reason I had to, but I still felt I'd wronged her somehow. Which was ridiculous, because she'd been waiting all week for a date that wasn't going to happen. The woman was fucking with my head.

I uncorked the wine and set the table. I'd even picked up flowers, knowing how crushed she'd be. I couldn't remember the last time I bought a woman flowers. The last time I'd care to, even. I put on a clean shirt and stared in the mirror, wondering if I should shave. I opted for no and went back down to wait for her.

By seven, I turned off the stove and figured she just wasn't coming home, which was crazy because by now everyone and their uncle was at home. I was just putting the sauce into a container when I heard her come in the front door.

"Lou!" I called, trying to sound cheerful. "Where the hell were you?"

"Next door," she said, coming into the kitchen and giving me a weak smile. "I stopped in for a glass of wine with Allie. I'm getting the feeling I won't be able to do that soon."

"Get the work-from-home order?"

"Yeah. If this lasts, I get the feeling there will be a lot more business for me."

She kicked off her shoes and came over to taste the sauce.

"Want me to put it back on? I could heat it up."

"No, thanks. Really not hungry." She paused, then said quietly, "I guess we can have it tomorrow night."

She was breaking my heart. I put down the container and turned to her.

"I'm so sorry, Lou. You'll get another chance, I promise. This won't last forever."

"Tell it to Italy."

I reached over and smoothed her hair.

"Will you stay?" she asked.

My heart stopped. What the fuck did she mean?

"What do you mean?"

She sighed and went to sit down. She put her feet up on the empty chair and had some wine.

"Look, I know you're anxious to get on with your life, but here's how I see it. Within days, we're going into lockdown. I don't want to do that alone. I was thinking we can turn the sunroom into a studio for you, move all that stuff into the basement. I can work in the dining room—I'd be out of your hair. We get along. Where are you going to go now?"

I sat down next to her. I couldn't believe my luck. Here I'd thought she wanted me out and she was scrambling for a way to get me to stay. If only she'd known.

"Are you sure?" I asked, trying to stay calm.

"Positive. I promise not to get in your way."

"Okay. I'll have my shit moved in tomorrow."

She smiled at me. I smiled back. I reached out and grabbed her hand, giving it a quick squeeze before letting go. I didn't want her thinking I was doing her a favour—she was the one doing me a solid. But I didn't know how to say it, so I said nothing. Just squeezed her hand.

*

Lou went up to bed pretty soon after that, clearly worn out by her day. I got to work bringing the boxes down to the basement. I wasn't wasting any time. I'd already called a few buddies to help me move my stuff out of storage and we'd set it up for the next morning. I worked until well past midnight clearing that room then mopped the floors and cleaned the windows. It was a great space. Tons of light, plenty of room for a work table and all my materials. It was close to four by the time I got to bed, and I crashed before my head hit the pillow.

I woke to the alarm a few hours later and leapt out of bed. I pulled on a pair of jeans and went to meet the guys. After a few trips back and forth, we'd managed to get everything into the sunroom before Lou even came down for breakfast. Granted, she didn't come down until noon. I made a mental note to keep an eye on her.

"What? What's going on?" she asked, looking around in amazement.

"Figured I'd get shit done before the lockdown hit," I said, shrugging.

A huge smile broke out across her face, and I mean, ear-to-fucking-ear. Any doubts I may have had about her wanting me to move in were gone. She was thrilled. I grinned back at her, probably looking like an idiot. She wandered into the sunroom, looking around. I hadn't had the chance to lay everything out yet, but the potential was plain to see. She came back out and gave me a quick hug.

"I'm glad," she said.

Then she walked away.

CHAPTER THIRTEEN

Louisa

By Friday afternoon, pretty much everyone was home and there for the long haul. Public gatherings were being limited and restrictions put in place, but most people were already bunking down. Toilet paper became incredibly difficult to find. I was thankful for my hoarding tendencies. For once.

By the time I came down for dinner, Ian had finished setting up his studio. He was standing in the kitchen, heating up the pasta bolognese. His black T-shirt was covered in dust and his ripped jeans had streaks of paint. He'd never looked better. He looked up when I entered and I smiled, praying he couldn't read my mind.

Truth was, I was pretty depressed. That

night was supposed to have been my first date since the divorce. My first time out with a man. My first opportunity to get laid. I had already decided that whether I liked the guy or not, I would sleep with him. Having Ian around had set my libido into overdrive, and if I didn't get some relief soon, I knew I'd be in trouble. The vibrator just wasn't cutting it anymore.

I sat down at the table just as he brought me my plate. Again, I smiled up at him but I could tell from the look in his eyes, he knew my heart wasn't in it. He sat down opposite me and took my hand.

"What's the matter, Lou?"

"It's nothing, really. Just the whole thing with Joel...Feels like just as I start getting my life together, this pandemic set in. Is that a sign or what?"

He was slowly massaging my hand and it was hella distracting. I shifted slightly in my seat, that now very familiar feeling starting to spread between my legs.

"It's not a sign. Don't be stupid. You will get to date. You will find the right person. Lou, you're amazing. I promise things will work out for you."

I burst into tears. I had no idea why. He was just being so sweet, so kind. And I just felt so hopeless. After all this time I'd finally put myself out there and this was how it ended up, with me crying at my kitchen table.

"Hey. Hey, Lou, stop that."

Ian dropped from his chair and knelt in front of me, taking both my hands now in his. He tugged on them gently until I raised my head and met his gaze.

"Don't cry. You're breaking my fucking heart."

I looked at him, so scrumptious and muscular, right there in front of me. A strong man. A real man. But it was Ian. My best friend. My vagina didn't care. She was all on board, pulsing at a hundred beats per second. I closed my eyes, thinking if I could get him out of my sight, I'd return to reality. When had this lusting started?

"Lou. Look at me."

I opened my eyes and looked at him. He was gazing at me with the softest eyes, filled with compassion and maybe some pity, but at this point, I didn't care. I'd take a pity fuck. I was that far gone. And then I had to laugh at the thought that Ian would ever even contemplate sleeping with me. He who had his warm body in every port, who slept with models and various other beautiful, uncomplicated, women. My laugh turned into a howl and when I looked back at him, he had the strangest look in his eye.

"What's so funny, Lou?"

"Nothing. Everything. Why don't you pour the wine?"

He looked at me again, then released my hands into my lap and stood. He walked over to retrieve his plate and the bottle of wine. He poured us both a glass and then sat down again. My breathing had returned to somewhat normal, but I was extremely conscious of the rise and fall of my breasts. I kept my face down in my plate, but felt his eyes on me and couldn't help but blush. I tried to focus on eating. And drinking. By the time I'd finished my plate, I'd already polished off two glasses of wine and was working on my third. Ian was still watching me closely.

When he got up to clear the plates, I stood, too. I wasn't sure what my plan was, but once I was on my feet, it was too late to sit back down. I didn't want to go upstairs, so I just kind of stood there with my drink in my hand, feeling awkward. He looked over at me and smiled.

"I'll clean up. Grab the wine and go to the living room. I'll be there in a minute."

I did as told.

I settled into the end of the sofa, curling up against the arm. I sipped my wine and looked over at the sunroom. The smell of fresh paint was more pronounced than in the kitchen, but it didn't bother me. It was another sign of change, of a new beginning. Despite my date not working out, things were still moving forward. I was beginning to hope the pandemic would stretch into the summer, just so I'd have the company.

Ian walked in and sat down at the other end of the couch. Way too far for a foot rub. I frowned and took another sip of wine. When I looked over at him, he was still studying me with that funny look.

"What is it, Lou? Tell me."

I sighed and took yet another sip, draining my glass. I reached forward for a refill and Ian put out his glass. I topped him up, too, then put the bottle down, settling back and taking a long sip.

"You hadn't even met the guy. Maybe you wouldn't have liked him."

I looked him straight in the eye.

"But I would've had sex."

Ian swallowed. He took a long sip of wine then put down his glass.

"You're lonely."

"Of course, I'm fucking lonely. I haven't been touched by a man in close to seven years. Can you even imagine what that feels like? Of course, you can't. You had sex a couple of nights ago."

"I did not."

"Whatever. I'm sure it hasn't been seven years."

"No. It hasn't. And no, I can't imagine. And I can't for the life of me figure out why you've made that choice. You're a beautiful woman, Lou. You're smart as hell, charming, witty, and great company. And look at you. You're forty and you're as hot as you were when you were sixteen."

"Shut up."

"I fucking swear to God, Lou."

I took another sip. He was a good friend. He'd say anything to make me feel better at this point, even tell me the 16-year-old nerd with glasses was hot. Fresh tears welled in my eyes and powerless to do anything, I felt one slide down my cheek.

Before I knew what was happening, Ian was beside me, taking the glass from my hand and putting it on the table. Then he took my face in his huge hand, so big I'm sure it was larger than my head. He reached with his thumb and wiped the tear from my cheek, then ran it along my bottom lip. I stared at him, confused. *Ian*. Yet the blood was running hot through my veins, radiating from the points where his skin made contact with mine. My breath caught as his thumb pulled my lip down slightly, stroking the moist interior.

Then he leaned in and kissed me. *Ian*. It wasn't like the kiss from the other night. It wasn't like any kiss I'd ever had. In fact, if I'd have known kissing was like *that*, I definitely wouldn't have gone seven years without it. His lips against mine were soft and forceful, hungry. There was a need I couldn't understand but wasn't prepared to resist. He ran his tongue along my bottom lip, and I parted my lips to invite him in. He moved closer to me and wrapped his free arm around my waist, pressing me against him.

My head was swimming. My nipples hardened against his chest and my arms automatically went around his neck. I kissed him back but let him take the lead, showing me all the incredible things he could do with his tongue. He groaned deep in his throat and it raised a thrill that ran throughout my entire body. *I did that.* I wrapped my fingers in his hair and he bit my lip, groaning again as I pressed further into him. *Ian*. Finally, he pulled away and looked at me.

"Is this okay?" he asked.

"Oh, Mac…"

"Say my fucking name, Lou."

I looked at him, confused. Then realization

hit me, and a slow smile crept across my face. I reached up and caressed his cheek.

"Ian."

He grunted and moved in on me again, taking my face in both hands and kissing me deeply, thoroughly. And again, hungrily, with need. *Where was this coming from?* He said he hadn't slept with that woman the other night. Maybe she'd left him wanting? I knew it was horrible, but I honestly didn't care. A bottle of wine in, seven years out, and a man who knew how to kiss in a way I never knew possible. I wasn't letting this opportunity pass me by. *This* was grabbing life by the balls.

His hands dropped to my waist and with seeming effortlessness, he lifted me and brought me onto his lap so I was straddling him. I draped my arms over his shoulders as he kissed my lips, my cheek, my neck. I sighed and let my head fall back as his hands moved down my back, stopping at my ass and resting there. He nuzzled my cleavage just above the V-neck of my shirt and I moaned, shifting myself in his lap until I was right on top of him. And he was *hard.* Like, rock-solid. He brushed his lips against my ear.

"You sure, Lou?"

"Shut up, Ian."

I kissed him again, and as it deepened, I

couldn't help but grind against him. He was just so hard, and I was so ready. His groan turned to a growl and his hands moved to my hips, pressing me down and stopping me from moving. I broke away and looked at him.

"What's wrong?"

"This can't go too far."

"You're right about that," I said.

"I'm serious, Lou. You're drunk. I'm drunk. We've been friends for twenty-five fucking years. I don't want to fuck that up."

"Oh, Christ, Ian."

I felt his cock twitch when I said his name. I slowly started to move against him again, knowing at least his body was on my side.

"Lou—"

"I'm so horny, Ian."

"Okay, maybe stop saying my name."

I leaned in and kissed him again, not caring if I was making a fool of myself. The steel rod against my thigh told me all I needed to know about what he wanted. He kissed me back, wrapping his arms around my lower back as I continued to grind against him. He pulled away again.

"You've got to stop doing that."

"You pulled me up here."

"Who *are* you?"

"Who are *you*?"

We stared at each other for what felt like forever. I had no idea what it was doing to him, but it was just cranking up the heat tenfold for me. His eyes were positively smoldering. He'd always been gorgeous, but right at that moment, I envied every one of those women in every one of those ports. *He'd been kissing them? Like the way he'd just kissed me?*

"Are you going to sleep with me?" I asked him, point-blank.

He shook his head slowly.

"Are you going to touch me?"

Again, he shook his head. Then he reached up and pulled my face down, kissing me again.

"I'm sorry," he whispered.

"Don't be," I said, trying to brush it off. "I'm sure you're not missing much. I've probably forgotten how to do all that stuff anyway."

He closed his eyes and let out a deep breath. I climbed off his lap and looked around awkwardly. I reached for my glass and took a slow sip. I smiled at him over my glass.

"I think I'm going to turn in."

"Lou—"

"It's okay, really. I get it. And I appreciate it. It's good that one of us has a head on their shoulders."

I gave him a half-hearted smile and fled to my room.

*

I shut the bedroom door behind me, leaning back against it until I could catch my breath. *Holy shit.* I'd momentarily managed to put the humiliating parts of the evening out of my head so I could focus on the *hot* part. I had kissed Ian. He'd kissed me. *Passionately.* Like he'd wanted me. *Me.*

I slowly walked over to my bed, peeling my clothes off as I went. I stopped at my night table, opening the drawer and rifling through until I found the right tool for the job, the only tool for the job—my magic wand. I leaned over to plug it in and crawled into bed. I knew it was loud, but Ian was still downstairs. No way he'd hear it from there, and in the state I was in, I figured it wouldn't take me long at all.

His lips. *Holy fuck.* The softest lips I'd ever felt against my own. My ex had been a lip-crusher. He'd never mastered the art of making out, seeing it as a necessary, tedious step between saying hello and fucking. He'd been the definition of wham-bam-thank-you-ma'am, which is why the affair always shocked me. He was interested in sex? Really? Turns out he was. Just not with me.

I pulled up the covers with one hand while I

turned on the magic wand with the other. I slid it between my legs and wrapped my thighs around it, creating as much pressure as possible. My hips rose off the bed as my head fell back onto the pillow. The intense pleasure raced through my body, causing my nipples to stand at attention. I closed my eyes, picturing Ian's mouth closing around them, licking, sucking. I moaned, shifting as I imagined his hands traveling between my legs, spreading my thighs.

I came violently, throwing my hand over my mouth to muffle my cries. I kept the wand in place, coaxing a second, even more intense orgasm from my body before finally settling back into the bed. I put the wand down beside me, not even bothering to unplug it, and rolled over and went to sleep.

CHAPTER FOURTEEN

Ian

I leaned back on the couch and closed my eyes. *Fuck.* Making out with Louisa Taylor had been even hotter than my wildest dreams. My dick was rock solid, remembering the feel of her grinding up against it. I heard the click and buzz break the silence. I could hear the vibrator from downstairs. Must be a magic wand. That's the only thing that made that much noise. I couldn't deny the bullshit male pride I felt at causing her to break out the big guns. The grin nearly split my face in two.

*

Despite the hangover, I was up at the ass crack of dawn the next morning. I jumped out of bed, eager to get into the studio and get to work. I had a million different conflicting thoughts going through my head, and I just needed to keep my hands busy.

I spent the first couple of hours organizing shit and setting up a work table. Then I pulled out the clay and filled a bowl with water and started playing around. I hadn't decided where I was going with my next piece, and I always started with clay before committing to anything real.

As my hands worked over the clay, relaxing and smoothing it as I went, my mind drifted back to the previous night. I had never meant to kiss her, but damn, I didn't regret it. She was just so sad, and I hated seeing her like that. Did she really not get what an amazing woman she was? How any guy would be lucky to have her?

And then the way she'd responded. Like she'd wanted it. Like she'd wanted *me*. Right. *Don't go there, asshole.* I had to keep reminding myself that her desire had nothing to do with me, and everything to do with close to seven years of deprivation. My dick couldn't even begin to comprehend that. No wonder the woman had a selection of vibes.

But what would happen now that we'd made out like horny teenagers? What was going to happen when she came down those stairs and into the dining room? Would I even be able to look her in the eye? Was she going to be pissed at me for taking advantage of her? *Fuck.* That thought hadn't even crossed my mind.

I grabbed my earbuds off the table and plugged them into my ears, cranking up the music on my phone. A little AC/DC would help drown out the confusion.

CHAPTER FIFTEEN
Louisa

I had no idea how long I sat at that table, watching Ian work through the glass door that separated the dining room from his studio. The way his large hands skimmed over the clay, smoothing and forming it. Then he'd dip his fingers in the water and repeat the whole process. I had to stay focused, because every time my mind drifted, I pictured him running those hands over my breasts. That was not a good road to travel down.

He was completely obvious to my presence as I sat there, drinking my tea and watching him. He had his earbuds in, yet I could still hear the faint streams of heavy metal music wafting through the room. It must've been loud. His leg was shaking in time to the music as his head bobbed up and down, his hands never stopping, as if they had a mind of their own.

I remembered how those hands felt cupping my face as he kissed me and suddenly I felt faint. I cringed inwardly as I thought about how I'd shamelessly ridden him, fully clothed, as if he were some sort of beast. Which I was beginning to suspect he was, but that was another story. He must have thought me so desperate. He was clearly struggling for a way to let me down easy, but the way he kissed me, how *hard* he'd been. I didn't understand how those two went hand in hand.

I had no idea what would happen when he noticed me sitting there, when we'd be forced to confront each other. I was sure he regretted last night. Clearly, it had been pity, but I'd jumped all over it and I was mortified by my behaviour. What if he wanted to move out? Although by the looks of it, he seemed quite comfortable where he was. I sat there for hours and he never got up to take a break, never stopped to eat.

After a while, a form emerged from the clay. From where I sat, it looked like a woman's buttocks—firm, round, ample. If that's what it was, it was beautiful, but watching him run his hand over it again and again was turning me on even more than I already was. Eventually, he picked up a knife and used one hand to carve and shape, while his other thumb smoothed over the clay in its wake. I was mesmerized and had to shift in my seat every time his thumb slipped underneath the sculpture, almost able to feel it skimming across my own sex.

I shifted in my seat and picked up my phone to check the time. Five o'clock. Holy shit. I had spent the entire afternoon watching him. I got up to stretch my legs and walked to the front door. I grabbed my coat and went out onto the front porch to get some air.

Outside, a bunch of the neighbours had congregated on their own porches, everyone holding a drink. I hadn't been standing there two minutes before Zach from two doors down walked over and held out a six-pack of beer bottles. I slid one out of the sleeve and smiled.

"Thanks, Zach."

"My pleasure," he said, and backed away.

I popped open my beer and took a long swig. It was a pleasant surprise, finding life outside and being offered the beer. I think Zach and I had exchanged maybe three words since he moved in a few years back. All I knew about him was that he was divorced and had lost custody of his two kids. Drugs or something. He was in the music industry, so it was probably a safe bet. The other thing I knew about him was that he was incredibly hot. Tall, built, and heavily covered in tattoos. Not my type, but at this point, I'd have jumped him in a heartbeat.

Which is maybe why I noticed that when he went back to his own porch, Casey was standing there waiting for him. I turned to find Allie, and catching her eye, raised my eyebrows at her. She smiled and shrugged. Casey was a 27-year-old lost soul who was house-sitting for the year while the Wexlers figured out what to do with their house. She was adorable, and everyone seemed to like her, but what the hell was she doing with Zach? There must have been at least eight years between them. Though did that even matter anymore?

My phone buzzed and I pulled it out of my pocket to look at it.

So? What's going on? I'm dying over here.

I smiled and looked up to see Allie staring at me, a plaintive look on her face. I rolled my eyes and walked down my front steps. She followed suit and we met on the sidewalk. Keeping the requisite two metres, we went for a quick walk down the block.

"So? SO?"

"Allie, I don't know. It's great having him around. It really is. But I'm so fucking horny all the time. I see him come out of the shower, I see him working out, and now today I watched him sculpt. It's ridiculous. This is my best friend."

"Best friend, my ass," Allie muttered under her breath.

"I heard that. Anyway, I'd been hoping to get some relief with that date, and then this freaking virus. I'm just so wound up."

She looked at me and cocked her head.

"Any chance of a friends-with-benefits situation?"

I debated telling her about the previous night, but I didn't want to give her any ammunition in her fight to get us together. I knew that was never happening. I shook my head.

"Doubt it. How's it going over at your place?"

A slow smile spread across Allie's face, and to be honest I felt a little dirty just looking at her.

"That good, huh?"

She nodded. "That good."

"Lucky you."

She shrugged and looked at me.

"You could—"

"Enough."

She laughed and we turned back toward the courtyard. By the time we got back, I saw Ian standing on the porch with his own beer in hand. He was laughing and talking across the lawn with Zach. We were too far away to hear the exchange, but both of them were smiling and nodding frantically. Then Ian looked around and his eyes landed on me. The smile vanished and my heart stopped. I heard my breath catch.

"Best friend, my ass," Allie repeated.

I turned to her, desperate, suddenly wishing I'd told her about the steamy make-out session.

"You don't understand—"

"Lou!" Ian called.

I turned and smiled at him, catching Allie's quizzical look before turning away. But it was too late. There was no escape now. I couldn't vanish into Allie's house. I had to go home. I was bound to home. To Ian. I took a deep breath and walked up my front stairs.

"Hey," I said.

"Hey. Where you been all day?"

I laughed.

"Watching you work," I said, the words out of my mouth before I could stop them.

He gave a little half-laugh, as if he wasn't sure whether or not I was joking. I opted not to clarify.

"Getting to know the neighbours?" I asked.

"I am. What a great bunch of people. How lucky you are."

"Yeah, well, I don't really know most of them," I said quietly.

He looked at me, confused.

"Why the fuck not?"

I shrugged.

"I told you. I've kind of kept to myself these past years."

He shook his head again and reached out to tousle my hair, but stopped, his hand hovering over my head. He pulled back awkwardly and looked around at the courtyard. *Great. He can't even bring himself to touch me now.*

"I'm going to go make some dinner," I said, moving past him toward the door.

"I thought that was my job."

"You stay out here. Get acquainted. I can handle dinner for a night."

I smiled at him and went inside.

CHAPTER SIXTEEN

Ian

A few weeks passed as I buried myself in my work. I locked myself in that studio from dawn to fucking dusk, and often beyond, in an effort to block out what was going out in the rest of the house. Everywhere I turned, there was Lou. I could hear her, see her, or smell her at any point during my day. It was killing me. But I didn't want to leave. I just had to figure out how to live with it.

We'd managed to avoid talking about that night. I mean, I knew I could avoid it. I'd spent my whole life not talking about shit. But I had no clue a woman could avoid it. But she did. The first couple of days were weird, but after that, we fell into this new routine of her working from home and me sequestering in the studio.

I'd decided to stick with the clay for the piece. My original intent had been to carve it out of marble, but I had bonded with this thing and I wasn't ready to let it go. It felt exactly how I imagined Lou's ass would feel in my hands. If it was all I had, I was keeping it.

We got through the days and then usually had a drink outside with her neighbours. What a crew she had out there. An odd mix, but fucking A when it came to interesting company. Zach reminded me a lot of me in my younger years. I loved shooting the shit with that dude.

Then we'd have dinner, but we never really hung out afterward like we did in the first weeks. I missed it, but at the same time, I was glad. I had no idea how I'd be able to keep my hands off her. I knew she was horny. I've been with enough women to know the signs. I could practically smell it coming off her. And God knows I wanted her, but when I took her, I wanted it to be because she was mine. Not because she had an itch to scratch and I just happened to be around.

But what I wouldn't have done just to kiss her again or make her come. Just once. I spent night after night lying in bed listening to that vibrator, jerking off to the sound of her moaning. I wanted to tear into that room, rip that thing out of her hand and bury my face between her thighs. I shook my head to clear it. *Get a fucking hold of yourself, man.*

I looked up and almost jumped out of my skin. Lou was standing right in front of me, holding two glasses of scotch. I swallowed and smiled at her, but I was stunned. She'd never once set foot in here.

"I'm sorry to bother you, Ian. Really. But I need to talk to you about something."

I reached out and took the glass from her. I took a swig, set it down, and picked up the clay. *Just keep your hands busy, man.*

"It's just that, well, the other night…"

And there it was.

"Well, it's just that. Ian. It's been a long time since I've had a man in the house, and it's just stirred up some…things for me."

"Lou, you don't have to explain. I wanted to —"

"Just let me talk, Ian. It's just that I never meant for anything —"

I caught her glance down towards my hands, which were absently working their way over the clay. I set the sculpture aside and gave her my full attention.

"I never meant for anything like that to happen. I know we're just friends. And your friendship means so much to me. I've missed you so much."

I stood up, practically knocking over my stool.

"I've missed you, too, Lou, I—"

"Dammit, Ian, just let me finish. I have a proposition."

And then she looked at me, her eyes searching mine, and I could practically see her brain trying to form the words. I knew what she was going to say. From talking to Zach, I knew the Wexler place was empty since Casey was shacking up with him. I'd have bet my life that Lou had arranged for me to move in there. *Fuck*. I never should have kissed her. What was I thinking?

And then her lips were on mine, her tongue working its way into my mouth. Stunned, I wrapped my arms around her waist, pulled her in close, and kissed her back. *What the fuck?* I drew away.

"What the fuck, Lou? What's going on?"

She just looked at me and sighed.

"I'm horny, Ian. I'm fucking horny. And I can't find a delicate way to say it."

She pulled away, leaving me completely dumbfounded. All the blood in my veins rushed towards my dick and before I knew it I was breathing heavily, staring at her and picturing her naked, on her back, just waiting for me. I shook my head. *No.*

"What are you saying, Lou?"

She took a deep breath and turned back to look at me.

"I know we're friends. I don't want to ruin that. But I don't know how long we're going to be quarantined here and I need to get off. And if you're going to be here, and I'm going to be here, I don't see why we can't lay some simple ground rules and work out some kind of friends-with-benefits situation."

I stared at her, still dumbstruck. I couldn't even form words.

"I would never have suggested it, trust me," she continued. "In a million years, I wouldn't have thought you could be attracted to me. But Ian." She glanced towards my dick, which was all the evidence either of us needed.

I coughed and tried to adjust myself discreetly. No luck. But I still couldn't speak.

She nodded.

"Okay. I get it. I just thought...And I just hope that you won't feel too weird living here now. I want you to stay. Really. I see you working in here, and it's just...right."

She turned to go and I reached and out grabbed her arm. I may not have had the words, but I knew how to act. I pulled her towards me and kissed her, long and deep. I felt her melt against me as her arms reached up and wrapped around my neck. Every thought I'd had moments earlier about not going down this road flew from my brain. I had Louisa Taylor in my arms. And then she pulled away.

"What are the rules," she asked, breathless.

"No intercourse," I said, thinking fast. "And you tell me when it gets weird."

She nodded.

"You'll do the same?"

I nodded and bent slightly, sliding my arm under her knees and lifting her up into my arms. Without another word, I carried her across the house, up the stairs into her room, and laid her down on her bed. I then knelt at her feet and peeled off her jeans, sliding them over her luscious hips and pulling them off one leg at a time.

"Ian," she said, looking down at me between her legs.

I looked up and met her gaze, and without breaking eye contact, bent my head and licked her from bottom to top. She cried out and threw her head back on the pillow. I smiled to myself, spread her thighs with my hands, and got to work.

The woman couldn't keep still. Nor could she keep quiet. It was such a turn-on going down on her. Never had I been with someone so fucking responsive. I didn't know if it was me, her, or the fact that no one had touched her in so long, but she had lost total control. And it was *hot*. She was screaming my name, and this time I was right there with her, not jerking off in my own room. *I did this.*

"Ian! Oh my god, I'm going to come…"

I slid my hands under her ass and squeezed, her hips rising off the bed as she rode my face. She came all over me, grinding against me, my tongue still deep inside her. I waited for her to come down, stroking her softly with my finger, smiling up at her and waiting for her to open her eyes.

"Look at me," I whispered.

She did. I smiled and she smiled back. I increased the pressure of my hand between her legs and watched with satisfaction as her smile transformed into something else completely. Before I knew it she was panting, writhing beneath my hand, and I could feel another orgasm building. She came loudly again, squeezing her thighs around my hand. I could've done this all fucking night.

In fact, I was about to go in for a third round when I felt her hands on my shoulders, pulling me up toward her. I glanced up at her, and she was shaking her head, breathless.

"I can't, Ian. No more."

"Of course you can," I said, shimmying down again.

She reached out again to stop me.

"I'm serious," she laughed. "My legs feel like Jello. Give me a minute."

I scrambled up the bed to lie down next to her. I ran my hand through her hair, separating the strands and just relishing the fact that I got to do this. I couldn't believe it. I half-expected to wake up at any moment, so I was taking full advantage of the situation.

She reached down shyly towards my belt. Despite my dick straining to reach her, I put out my hand and stopped her. She looked up at me, puzzled.

"What's wrong?" she asked.

"Not tonight. Tonight's for you. Seven fucking years, Lou."

"A lifetime, Ian."

I looked at her. *What?*

"What do you mean, a lifetime? What does that even mean?"

She swallowed and looked at me.

"Let's just say he was never that much into foreplay. More of a wham-bam-thank-you-ma'am kind of guy."

I stared at her, stunned. Was she trying to tell me no one had ever gone down on her before?

"I mean, he touched me, of course. But he just felt that oral sex was a bit…ick."

I thought I was going to pass out. She had the sweetest pussy I'd ever tasted. Just hearing this was driving me insane. She looked at me and laughed nervously.

"So…Thank you, I guess?"

I leaned over and kissed her, pushing her back onto the bed as I worked my way down her body again. She protested weakly but fell silent the moment my tongue hit her clit. And then a whole new type of noise started.

*

I finally left her, a couple of orgasms later, passed out in her bed. I stood up and stared at her. The woman had literally passed out from pleasure. She was a goddess and I felt like a god. I adjusted my pants, second-guessing my decision to not let her touch me, and walked out of the room.

I went downstairs and turned on the kitchen light, rummaging in the fridge for the orange juice. Knocking back a glass, I continued to my studio and sat down. It was pitch black in there, so I turned on the small desk lamp. I reached over and picked up the sculpture and my knife. Remembering the exact feel of her ass in my palm, I made corrections as my hands moved over the clay. I was lost in the work and didn't hear her come in. I jumped when I felt her hand on my shoulder.

I looked up at her and smiled. She was wearing her T-shirt and nothing else. She didn't say a word, but reached over and gently took the clay from my hands and put it on the table. She looked at it for a moment, then smiled at me again. She pushed back my stool and climbed onto my lap, facing me. She draped her arms loosely over my shoulders and leaned in to kiss me. I took her head in my hands and fisted her hair as I kissed her back. She moved up on my lap, sitting directly on my growing cock. I groaned and she started to grind.

"Lou—"

"Shhh—"

She tightened her grip on my shoulders and increased her speed until she was riding me, her bare-assed, me still in my jeans. I grabbed her hips and breathed into her neck, pulling at her collar with my teeth to kiss her shoulder. She moaned, causing me to growl in return. I pulled her in closer, her tits crushed up against my chest. She cried out and before I knew it, she was coming in my lap, and I wasn't far behind her. I pushed her down onto my cock, grinding against her until I felt my own release. I collapsed against her, holding her waist like an anchor.

She kissed the top of my head, got up, and walked out. I listened as she crossed the house and went up the stairs.

What the fuck?

CHAPTER SEVENTEEN
Louisa

"Honestly? It's like this fog has been lifted. Like I can finally see things clearly again," I said.

I was taking my daily socially-distanced walk with Allie and filling her in on the previous night's activities. She was eating it up. I had never realized that sharing these experiences with close friends was almost as good as having them. I'd been learning a lot during the pandemic. She laughed.

"The power of a good orgasm. Clears things right up for you."

"It really does," I said, still marveling.

"How'd he compare?" Allie asked, a mischievous gleam in her eye.

I shrugged.

"Couldn't tell you. First time."

Allie stopped so fast I thought she'd fallen down. She just stared at me, much in the same way Ian had when I told him, minus the lust.

"No one has ever gone down on you before?"

"Not before last night."

"Well, holy fuck. How does that even happen, Louisa?"

I shrugged again and started walking, slowly while I waited for her to catch up.

"I don't know. My ex wasn't into it. And I was a nerd in high school. I never even dated, much less had a boyfriend. It just never happened."

Allie shook her head slowly, still digesting this information.

"That must have been…earth-shattering for you," she said.

"It was!!"

We both laughed and walked some more, turning the corner back onto our block.

"So what does this mean?" she asked after a while.

"Nothing. We laid down the ground rules. No intercourse, no getting weird around each other. I haven't seen him since I molested him in his studio last night, so I'm not sure how that second rule is going to go, but I guess it's 'wait and see' at this point."

"You don't have to wait much longer."

Allie nodded discreetly towards my front porch, where Ian was waiting with two cups of tea and a smile. I looked at Allie and raised my eyebrows, then trotted up my front steps. I took the cup from him and returned the smile. He leaned in close until his forehead was touching mine. My breath caught.

"No weirdness," he whispered.

I burst out laughing and he tousled my hair. I smiled up at him and continued into the house. He stayed behind to chat with Allie for a bit while I went up for a shower. By the time I came down, he was sitting in the kitchen, eating a sandwich.

"Want me to make you something?" he asked.

I swallowed and stared at him, watching his mouth close around the bread, flashbacks of the previous night whipping through my head. I took a deep breath and gave him a shaky smile.

"I'm good, thanks. The tea is perfect. I had a late breakfast."

I sat down next to him and picked up the magazine from the table. *Sculpture Magazine.* I flipped through the pages, pausing here and there to study the works of art. Ian ate and watched me—I was conscious of his eyes on me the entire time. My pulse quickened and it was getting difficult to breathe.

"Lou. No weirdness."

I looked up at him and closed the magazine.

"You're right. Sorry."

He smiled and nodded, taking a sip of his drink.

"Thank you," I said.

"For what?"

I laughed.

"Um...for last night? It was pretty spectacular."

He grinned so wide it lit up his eyes. I watched the creases form around them, and his mouth, and squirmed a little in my seat. *Louisa. It's noon. Calm yourself.*

"Was it now?"

"Don't be a dick, Mac."

He glared at me.

"Ian. Sorry."

He smiled, softening.

"Lou, I'm happy to be of service. Seriously. You snap your fingers, I'm there. I'd been wondering how I could repay you for your generosity, seeing as you won't take rent money from me."

"Room and board in exchange for orgasms?"

He shrugged.

"And studio space. I've made worse deals."

I laughed.

"Listen, Lou. I heard you last night. Nothing serious. I get it. You're here, I'm here. I think as long as we know where the lines are drawn, it'll be fine. You're smoking hot in bed, by the way."

My belly did a flip-flop and I felt a lightning bolt of heat strike between my legs. No one had ever said that before. No one. Ha. My ex. My ex had never said that before. Then again, I don't remember making nearly as much noise with him as I did with Ian last night. I couldn't keep still. Everywhere he touched me lit up, spreading fire through my veins.

"I know you don't believe me," he said. "But it's true. Say the word and I'll drop to my knees right now."

His words hit every erogenous zone in my body at once. I shifted in my seat, suddenly very warm and extremely uncomfortable. I felt myself blushing but was powerless to stop it. He made a move to get up and I laughed, putting out my hand.

"Ian. It's fine. Really."

He raised his eyebrows and shrugged.

"Anytime, babe."

*

Later that night, I was on my way up to bed and I passed by Ian's door. It was slightly ajar and I caught a glimpse of him lying on his bed, wearing only his pajama pants, reading. He heard me go by, looked up, and smiled. I smiled back and hurried on. I stopped outside my door, but I knew if I went into my room, I was pulling out a battery-operated friend. *And really, why should I?*

I took a deep breath, turned around, and knocked on Ian's door.

"Yeah?" he said.

I walked in and he put his book down, carefully folding over the page first. He sat up against the headboard. I said nothing.

"What is it, Lou?"

I couldn't bring myself to speak to the words. To tell him what I wanted. I had figured he'd know, just by the act of me walking into his room at 11:30 at night. I looked up at him, shyly, trying desperately to convey what I was thinking with my eyes. A look passed over his face as he took me in, then he moved over on the bed and patted the space beside him. I walked over.

"You don't have to be shy with me, Lou."

I sat next to him and he reached over, stroking my hair, tucking it behind my ear.

"Ian—"

"I'm serious. We've got an arrangement. I'm cool with it. Trust me."

He leaned in toward me and all my apprehensions flew out the window. I let him kiss me, opening myself to him as he explored with his tongue. He bit my lower lip and drew away, looking me in the eye. I tried to catch my breath, but he was so close, and he smelled so good. Freshly showered with his hair still damp. I couldn't resist reaching up and running my hand through his curls, watching the droplets fall to his shoulder. I leaned over and licked one off. He groaned. I couldn't believe I'd never noticed the sexiness of him before, what a complete turn-on he was.

He put his hands on my shoulders and pushed me back against the headboard, never breaking contact with my lips. I wrapped my arms around his neck, letting him guide me into whatever position he wanted. From the moment he touched me, I was completely under his spell. He pulled away and slowly unbuttoned my blouse, taking his time to trace the skin beneath with his fingertips as he worked. I closed my eyes and sighed.

His hand worked beneath the fabric of my shirt as it found my breast. He cupped it in his hand, using his thumb to lightly stroke me through my bra. Every time he hit my nipple, I moaned, twisting on the bed and pressing my breast further into his hand.

"So fucking hot," he murmured, leaning down to kiss the base of my throat as his hands spread the front of my shirt apart. He drew back to look at me, shaking his head slowly and then lowering it again to kiss a trail between my breasts. I raised my hips, panting at this point, aching for him to touch me.

He paused at my navel, swirling his tongue and sending a shock wave of pleasure up my spine. I cried out and I felt him smile against the soft flesh of my belly. His hands worked upwards, his mouth following suit as he climbed his way back up my body. He propped himself up on his elbow, gazing down at me as he used one finger to lower each cup on my bra, one after the other until my breasts were exposed and completely at attention.

I closed my eyes once again as he leaned forward, taking my nipple in his mouth. *Fuck.* I grabbed his shoulders, digging my nails into his skin, feeling the muscle ripple underneath. He moved to my other breast, using his teeth to gently pull and tease, causing my hips to rise off the bed, my body pulsing with need.

"Ian...fuck. What the fuck..."

"Hmm. Language, Lou. I've never known you to use such language."

He grinned at me as moved up and kissed me.

"Clearly, that asshole never took proper care of you. It's my honour to rectify that."

With that, he reached down and undid my jeans, pulling them down over my hips and letting them gather at my knees. He slid his hand up between my thighs, stroking me lightly as he took my nipple back into his mouth.

"Oh, *fuck. FUCK.*"

"Lou, you're really turning me on with that shit. And you're so goddamn wet."

I blushed furiously, hoping he wouldn't notice in the faint light of the room. No luck. He pulled his hand away and lifted his head.

"Stop being embarrassed. I'm serious. You are fire. Own this shit. Look what you've done."

He reached for my hand and brought it down between his legs, pressing it up against the steel rod that had taken up residence in his pants. I groaned, rubbing him up and down as I rolled over to grind up against his leg. I slid my hand across his taut stomach and down into the waistband of his pajamas. He wasn't wearing underwear. I groaned again as I took him in my hand. He was so hard and so silky and warm. I reached up and kissed his neck, brushing my lips against his ear.

"Show me how to make you feel good," I whispered.

"That feels pretty fucking good, Lou."

"Ian. I'm forty years old and I don't know how to do this. Don't make me beg."

He turned to me.

"You serious?" he asked.

"I am. You're my best friend. Help me out."

I peered up at him and he leaned down to kiss me. Then he reached down and wrapped his hand around mine, both of us taking him firmly in our grip. I closed my eyes and leaned against his chest and we moved up and down together, stroking him, tugging, going up over the head and down again. He showed me how to rub the vein underneath, something I never even knew existed. But hearing him moan when I applied pressure was all I needed to understand how that little bit of anatomy worked.

More and more I was coming to realize how deprived of a healthy sex life I'd been. Foreplay wasn't a part of my marriage. It was all about his pleasure, and he wanted it fast and quick. The things Ian was doing, the things he was teaching me, and the way both our bodies responded—it was almost too much. I heard his breathing quicken and he took my hand

and placed them over his balls before he continued to pump.

"Feel this," he said.

Seconds before he came, I felt his balls constrict, tightening in my palm as the rest of his body tensed and then released. He moaned and I felt the wet, sticky liquid drip onto my hand. I looked up at him and smiled. He winked and I laughed.

"Good?" I asked.

"Fucking A, Lou."

I pulled my hand out of his pants and stared at it, looking at the droplets of come that remained. Curious, I brought my hand up to my mouth and took a tentative lick. I looked over at him and his eyes practically rolled back in his head.

"Fuck. Lou."

He pushed me back down on the bed and pulled my pants off the rest of the way, throwing them across the room. He climbed back up, laying on top of me, and looked into my eyes.

"Tell me what makes *you* feel good. What do you like?" he asked.

I smiled.

"Your face. Between my legs."

He gave me a quick salute before he disappeared.

CHAPTER EIGHTEEN

Ian

Part of me thought I'd hit the jackpot. Part of me honest-to-god thought I was in heaven. But the rest of me knew I was really in hell. If I'd have had this arrangement with any other woman in the world, it would've been one thing. But with Lou, it was pure torture.

I wanted her every minute of every day.

She just had to look in my direction and I was hard. I would sit in my studio all day, the one place I had always been able to focus and work, yet I could feel her eyes on me. And if she wasn't there, I could sense her presence in the house. It was killing me. Every single piece I worked on was a part of her anatomy. If she figured it out, she'd probably freak and ask me to move out.

We went on like that for a couple of weeks. Her walks got fewer and farther between as the seriousness of this crazy virus set in. We started ordering food online and frantically searching for toilet paper. We'd still go out for drinks on the porch occasionally, but the novelty had worn off and everyone was a little on edge. Except that little Catholic couple. They looked like two pigs who'd been rolling in shit all day. Face-splitting grins on their face 24/7. I could only imagine what was going on in their house.

One afternoon, Lou came over to the studio door and stood there. She didn't often come to visit me, something I appreciated. But when she did come, it was a rare treat. A ray of sunshine in my day. I looked up at her and smiled.

"Hey, Lou. What's up?"

She smiled.

"I just quit my job."

I stood up.

"What?"

"You heard me. I quit. Done. Finished. I mean, I have to close up my files and transfer some cases, but otherwise, I'm done."

I grabbed her and lifted her up before gathering her in for a hug. I rarely touched her first, always letting her make the first move, but this was different. This was life-changing.

"Lou! That's amazing! I'm so happy for you."

She smiled as I set her back down on the ground. She smoothed out her shirt and looked back up at me. She was adorable, gazing up at me beneath those lashes. I could feel the heat radiate between us. I had to look away. *It's just lust, man. Calm yourself.*

"What's next?" I asked.

"Unsure. I'm going to take some time during this pandemic and then maybe look for work in my field. My *real* field."

No words could've made me happier. Okay, maybe some words could've made me happier. *Fuck me, Ian.* Or, maybe *I love you, Ian.* But since neither of those was going to happen, I was glad to revel in her professional triumphs.

"I'm going to order dinner. Mexican from around the corner. You good with that?"

I nodded at her as she turned to go. She stopped at the door and looked over her shoulder at me.

"Thank you, Ian. You being here and giving me the confidence? It had a lot to do with my decision. Scratch that. It had everything to do with my decision."

Once again, I couldn't find the words. She turned and walked out.

*

Later, as we sat at the table unpacking the food, I grabbed a chip and dipped it into the salsa.

"That's the hot one," Lou warned me.

I laughed her off and popped the chip in my mouth. My eyes must've flown wide open because that shit *was* hot. Lou laughed at me, rightfully so, and passed me a piece of bread. I took it gratefully once I stopped coughing.

"I want you to get tested," she said.

I looked at her, confused.

"For Covid?" I asked. "I'm coughing from the heat."

She smiled and looked down.

"No. For STDs. I want you to teach me how to give head. But I want to know you're clean."

Well, fuck me. My dick certainly liked hearing that.

"Um, Lou, I hate to break it to you, but you've already—"

"I know," she said, interrupting me. "And don't think I haven't lost sleep over it."

I sat up and took her hands. I looked her straight in the eye.

"Don't. I'm clean. I get tested regularly. And I was tested right before I came here, after my last…encounter."

"What about that woman—?"

"I told you, Lou. I didn't sleep with that woman. She came on to me at a bar. I had no interest."

She nodded, considering. Then she looked me in that shy way she had, swallowed, and licked her lips.

"Ready to go upstairs?"

*

I brought her upstairs to my room, my heart slamming in my chest. I was so hard I worried I'd blow the moment she touched me. Just the thought of her lips wrapped around me—every teen-aged dream I'd had about her. Christ.

I turned to face her, both of us standing at the foot of my bed. I put my finger under her chin, tilting her head up towards me, and kissed her. I was gentle, trying to pace myself, not let her know how much I wanted this. I pushed her hair out of her face, smiling at her, trying to control my breathing.

I couldn't say the same for her. She was fucking panting.

"You nervous?" I asked.

She shook her head slowly.

"If at any point, you want to—"

"Shut up, Ian."

She dropped to her knees and worked the buckle on my belt. Then she undid my jeans, pulling them down over my hips and pushing them down to the floor. She took a moment to stroke me through my boxer briefs and I couldn't help but groan. She smiled up at me, and at the sight of her there on the ground, between my legs, I swear my dick grew two sizes. She lowered my underwear and tilted her head, considering my dick. I had no idea what was going through her mind, and I was not about to ask. Let the woman explore.

She reached out and stroked me, both of us mildly startled as my cock strained and jumped. She gave a soft laugh, then leaned in and gently put out her tongue, licking the head. My knees buckled and she reached out quickly, grabbing my hips. She drew away and turned slightly, guiding me to the edge of the bed, where I gratefully sat down.

Christ. There was no way I wasn't coming within five seconds.

She closed her lips around me and I went through the litany of shit reviews I'd had at previous shows, of failed pieces, of my grandfather, of anything that would take my mind off of what Louisa was doing to my cock. Jesus Christ. She was like a kid in a fucking candy store.

I put my hands on her head, then dropped them to her shoulders.

"Slow down, slow down."

She looked up at me, frowning.

"No good, huh? Shit. I'm just doing everything I ever wanted to do. Trying it all, you know? I guess I'm a little—"

"Lou, shut up. You're fantastic. But I don't want to blow yet."

Her lips curled up into a smile of satisfaction and it was the sexiest goddamn thing I'd ever seen. She took me in her mouth and every goddamn thing I taught her to do with her hand she repeated with her tongue. Christ, no wonder that woman did so well in school. She was a star pupil.

"Right there, Lou. Right underneath—with the tip of your tongue. Oh, fuck, yeah."

I felt the vibration along my cock as she laughed and I gripped her shoulders.

"Fuck. Lou. Try your teeth. Lightly! Yeah. Fuck, yeah. Just like that."

She dragged her teeth along the length of my cock and then swirled her tongue around the head before taking me in again, this time deep. She wrapped her mouth around me and I came violently, out of nowhere. I had *not* meant to come in her mouth on her first time.

"Christ, Lou, I'm so sorry."

She drew her head away, and used her thumb to wipe her bottom lip. She threw me this lazy, sexy-as-fuck smile.

"Delicious."

CHAPTER NINETEEN

Louisa

To say the first month of the pandemic was strange would be an understatement. Life as we knew it ceased to exist. We had already started referring to it as the Before Times. Instructions from health officials were changing daily, new restrictions put in place, old ones lifted. It was confusing and more than a little scary. I was glad to have Ian with me.

We spent a lot of time glued to YouTube, watching videos from Italy to see what was awaiting us. Parts of the country had been in lockdown for over a month already and it was completely surreal to hear what they had to say. We both fell into bread baking, a hobby people across the world seemed to be taking up. I think we were just grateful to have something to do with our hands during those long hours. Though I'd be lying if I said I wasn't having filthy thoughts while watching him knead. And he knew it. But still, weeks into our arrangement and he still refused to make the first move. It was always my call.

Part of me wished he'd just sweep me off my feet, take me by surprise, but then I remembered. This was satisfaction in return for room, board, and studio space. This was not romance. This was not love. This was Louisa and Ian, two best friends scratching a mutual itch.

So why did I get butterflies in my stomach every time he turned that gorgeous smile on me? And every time I closed my eyes, I pictured him drawing me close in bed after driving me over the edge, over and over. Yes, the dirty parts were awesome, but it was those after-moments of tenderness I was starting to crave. *Not good, Lou.*

I'd always known Ian was a great guy. He was my best friend, for Christ's sake. But now that I knew how sexy he was, how much we turned each other on, I couldn't fathom why we'd never made a go of it before. And then I remembered. He was Ian Mackenzie, world-renowned artist, and I was Louisa Taylor, lonely divorcée. He dated models and actresses. I slept with my vibrator.

It had been days since I'd seen or spoken to Allie. *That's what I need, a reality check.* When I sat down for breakfast one morning, I picked up my phone and texted her. She answered immediately. I grabbed my mug and within minutes we were both at the foot of the courtyard, heading down the street, two metres between us.

"What's up?" she asked.

I looked over at her. She was flushed. Her hair was tousled. I knew that look.

"You answered the phone mid-sex?" I asked.

"Post-sex. Forget me. What's up?"

"I think I made a mistake?"

She looked at me, studying my expression.

"He falling in love?" she asked.

I shook my head.

"I am."

Allie rolled her eyes.

"This is the first man you've been with since your divorce. Are you sure about that?"

"I think I am."

"And how does he feel about you?"

"What's the expression? Available pussy?"

Allie winced.

"Please."

"Allie, it's true. We're in a pandemic. He's shut up with me for god knows how long. Who else is he going to fool around with?"

"So you're still not fucking?"

"No. And it's killing me. I want him so badly."

"Have you told him?"

I looked at her, shocked.

"No! And I won't. We have an arrangement. He's sticking to it, so will I."

"He's sticking to it how?"

I smiled.

"He doesn't touch me until I make a move on him. He sees this as a service deal."

She rolled her eyes.

"I doubt it. You're an amazing woman, Lou. He came to see you after all this time. Give it a chance. I've gotten to know him a bit. He's a good man."

*

One night later in the week, we were lingering at the table after dinner, neither of us anxious to turn in. It had been a couple of nights since we'd fooled around. I had mentally put the brakes on while I tried to figure things out in my head. As much as I wanted him, I didn't want to get hurt in the process. I was so far gone by this point that I was spending hours of my day pretending to work while gazing at him over my laptop. The way his hands moved, how the muscles in his biceps rippled as he beat the clay into submission. Twice I had gotten off in the dining room, my hand working furiously under the table as I watched the curve of his shoulders as he reached for a tool hung high on the wall or the slope of his neck as he bent to carve out an intricate detail in his work.

Louisa. For fuck's sake.

I shook my head, trying to clear it, trying desperately to see through my lust haze. The air was so heavy between us. He had been polite and friendly and chatty the past week but had still made no move toward me. The most contact we'd had was when he tousled my hair, which was less and less frequently. He didn't even joke about it or slide in some comment in conversation. I had to assume he was fine *not* fooling around with me. That it truly was an arrangement, that he got nothing from it otherwise. It crushed me.

I looked up and saw he was staring at me. His breathing was heavy and he had both hands on the table, palms down. I couldn't tear my eyes away from his.

"What is it?" he asked.

I cocked my head and studied him, scanning his face, trying desperately to read him. No luck.

"I'm second-guessing my sex appeal," I said cautiously.

He raised his eyebrows and leaned forward.

"Elaborate, please."

I took a deep breath.

"I haven't come to your room in days, and you haven't even looked at me askance. I mean, I know this is a deal we brokered, but I thought things were pretty hot between us."

"Lou. Things are smoking hot between us."

"So—?"

It was his turn to take a deep breath.

"So I told you from the beginning. It's on your word. Always. I'm here. Don't think I don't want you."

He stood and I gazed down at him, seeing the evidence that he did, indeed, want me. Very badly from the looks of things. I swallowed.

"Take off your pants and sit on the table, Lou."

I turned to the table, momentarily distracted by the thought that we ate at that table. But he reached over and flicked my nipple and all rational thought left my brain.

"I said, take off your pants and sit on the table."

I stood and slowly peeled down my pants

and my panties, stepping out of them and climbing up onto the table.

"Take off your shirt. And your bra."

I looked around, checking to make sure no one could see in through the windows. Again he reached out and flicked my nipple, and again I forgot my concerns. I unbuttoned my shirt and unclasped my bra, letting both fall to the ground. He licked his lips and adjusted his pants.

"Lou, I want you to touch yourself. I want you to show me how you make yourself come."

My breath caught. I was naked, sitting on my kitchen table with all the lights on. This was not how I did things. I was suddenly very self-conscious and very turned on.

"Go on. Spread your legs for me."

"Why?" I managed to ask, so quietly I worried he wouldn't hear.

"Because I have jerked off to this scenario more times than I can count, Lou. I'm taking my opportunities where I can."

I had no idea what that meant, but the mere idea of him jerking off to *any* fantasy of me was enough to make me forget my apprehension and focus entirely on the wetness spreading between my legs. I pressed the palm of my hand against myself, closing my eyes as I felt the electric charge run through my clitoris. I moaned, and heard Ian's belt unbuckling, followed by the sound of his pants dropping to the floor.

My hand moved slowly, rubbing myself, savouring the feeling of building tension. I opened my eyes and looked at Ian. He was staring at me, eyes hooded with lust and his hand wrapped around his cock, stroking absently. I slipped one finger, then two, inside myself, tilting my hips to give Ian a better view. He growled in response, deep in his throat and with an animal-like quality. I moved my thumb over my clitoris, starting with slow circles and then rubbing frantically as I felt my orgasm build.

All this time, he just watched me, barely breathing and stroking himself lightly. It was so intense, neither of us saying a word, his eyes fastened between my legs, watching my hand work and my rising excitement.

"Christ, Lou."

That was all I needed. I exploded onto my hand, bright light and stars blocking out everything in my field of vision. I cried out, my ass slipping down the table as I supported myself with my other hand.

"Oh, fuck, yes. Fuck, yes," I cried.

Before I knew it, his mouth was on mine,

drowning out my cries. I wrapped my arms around him, kissing him furiously and with an urgency I couldn't explain. I'd *just* come, but I still wanted him, needed him.

I wrapped my legs around his waist and drew him towards me. He held my hips, pulling me even closer until his cock was rubbing up against me. I felt faint. We'd never both been naked below the waist before at the same time, for reasons which were rapidly becoming obvious. He continued kissing me, setting off sparks in my brain, tiny little fireworks that spread throughout my body. I felt the tip of his cock teasing my clit and pushed up against him.

His hands tightened on my hips and he drew back.

"No, Lou."

"Please, Ian, fuck the ground rules. We're grownups."

I knew I was just setting myself up for a world of hurt, but in that moment, there was nothing I wanted more than Ian Mackenzie inside me, fucking me every which way until Tuesday. He took my face in his hands and looked me in the eye.

"It's not going to happen, Lou. Forget it. There are ground rules for a reason."

"I know, I know, so I don't get hurt. I won't

get hurt. I promise you."

He dropped his hands and took a step backwards. He looked at me, a bittersweet smile on his face.

"No, Lou. It's so I don't get hurt. I love you, and if we sleep together and you walk away, it'll break my fucking heart."

With that, he leaned over, kissed me on the forehead, grabbed his pants, and went up the stairs.

CHAPTER TWENTY

Ian

I lay on my bed, naked and staring up at the ceiling. I'd said it. I'd said the words. But I honestly didn't care anymore. I couldn't pretend. I couldn't act like I didn't want her all the fucking time. It was killing me, watching her come night after night, knowing her pleasure had nothing to do with me, that any substitute would've sufficed.

I couldn't even think about what would happen the next day. The Wexler place was suddenly looking pretty damn appealing. How could I face her? I'd broken the ground rules. I'd let it get weird. Twenty-five years of friendship, flushed. *Fuck.*

I heard her approach and I flung the sheet over my midsection before she knocked.

"Come in," I said.

She pushed the door open slowly, then walked in. She was wearing her panties and her button-down shirt, only a few buttons done up here and there. In fact, the entire shirt was askew and I had to restrain myself from getting up and ripping it off her. Instead, I re-adjusted the sheet.

She sat down on the end of the bed and studied me. My heart dropped.

"What are you saying, Ian?"

"You heard me. You know damn well what I'm saying. I love you, Lou. I can't sleep with you because I fucking love you."

She closed her eyes and sat silently for a moment as if she were gathering her strength. Then she opened them and looked at me, but she wasn't really seeing me.

"You don't love me, Ian. I'm just here. We're stuck here together, confined for who knows how long? I'm a warm body, I fulfill a need. *Available pussy*, I believe it's called?"

Hearing her say those words made the blood pump in my ears. My heart was pounding. I was grinding my teeth, willing myself to let her fucking finish. But I was getting angry. How dare she tell me how I felt?

"And it's okay, really. I get it. I'm here. I'm not half-bad looking. You're comfortable with me. You trust me. I give decent head. And most of all, I guess, you feel like you're paying me back. Which is unnecessary, of course—"

As I listened to her, my anger faded. It was starting to sound very much like a rehearsed speech, like one she'd repeated to herself over and over again. *Is this what she had convinced herself was going on?*

"Shut the fuck up, Lou."

She looked at me, startled, as if seeing me for the first time. As if I'd interrupted her mantra. I looked around and saw my sweats on the edge of the bed. I reached for them and pulled them on, not wanting to distract either of us at that particular moment. I got out from beneath the sheet and slid over next to her on the bed. I took her head in my hands and turned her to face me.

"Lou. This has nothing to do with the pandemic. I have loved you since the moment you walked into that history classroom in that purple sweater and pink-rimmed glasses. I have loved you through every day of high school, college, and every day of my life since. When you got married, I had to walk away. I couldn't bear it. I fucked my way across Europe trying to forget you. And when I heard you'd left him, I had to come back."

She looked up at me, her eyes wide and

uncomprehending.

"Since high school?" she asked, the disbelief clear in her eyes.

"Since the very first time I laid eyes on you. And to tell you the god-honest truth, Lou, for a second that day, I thought you felt the same. The way you looked at me, the way our eyes locked…I fucking thought you felt the same."

"I did," she said quietly.

My gaze snapped up towards her. She raised her eyes to meet mine and swallowed.

"That very first day," she said. "But I knew who you were. I knew I never had a chance. So I pushed it away. And I was glad I did. Because we became friends."

"We became friends because I couldn't bear to lose you. Did you really think I was that stupid that I couldn't remember the dates for World War One? Jesus Christ, Lou. If friendship was the only thing you were offering, I was taking it."

Her eyes searched mine, still so confused.

"So why didn't you ever do anything? You never asked me out."

I sighed.

"I was an ass. I thought I had time. I thought I had all the time in the world. I was too insecure in high school, and by the time I'd worked up my nerve in college, you had hooked up with that asshole. I was too fucking late."

She stared at me, her face still cupped in my palms. I wanted to kiss her so badly, but I knew this was on her. She leaned her head towards me and it was all I needed. I pulled her in and kissed her, long and deep. She responded in kind, clutching at my hair as she twisted her body around and climbed into my lap. I drew away, running my thumb across her bottom lip.

"I need to hear it, Lou. I need to hear you say it."

"I love you, Ian."

I kissed her again, every fibre of my being reveling in the sensation of having her in my lap, in my arms. She moved in closer, rubbing up against me, and my dick grew hard, straining towards her. I groaned, low and deep, and clutched her tighter.

"I want you, Ian," she whispered, sliding her lips across my neck. I shuddered, and she reached out with her tongue, tracing a line up to my jaw.

I wound my hand in her hair at the nape of her neck, pulling her head back so she was forced to look at me.

"If I take you, Lou, you're mine."

She answered me with a kiss, pushing me

backwards onto the bed as she straddled me, then leaned down, pressing her tits against my chest. *Fuck this.* I reached in and ripped the shirt off, buttons flying in all directions. She let out a little laugh, which made me smile. She reached into my pants and took hold of my dick, who was very pleased with this turn of events. *Very* pleased.

She shimmied down my legs as she eased my pants over my hips. She dipped her head, snaking out her tongue to make a lazy circle around the head of my cock. It sprang up towards her, and she closed her mouth over me.

"Fuck, Lou."

She looked up at me, all innocent-eyed with my cock in her mouth. I groaned and dropped my head back on the pillow. I felt her mouth leave me as she continued up my body, rubbing herself along every hard surface she could find on the way. She sat back up and grinned down at me, an evil look on her face. She took my dick in hand and lazily dragged it against the opening of her pussy. Christ, she was wet.

"Lou—"

"It's okay, you're clean, remember?"

She rubbed the head of my cock against her clit, working herself into a good rhythm as I lay powerless beneath her, vowing to thrust a hand between us if she attempted entry. I reached up and cupped her tit, thumbing her nipple and giving it a squeeze and she threw back her head and screamed, coming all over me. My dick twitched, aching to get inside her.

When she came back down, she looked at me and smiled again. She resumed her hold on me, this time guiding me inside. *Oh, no.* I reached down, forming a barrier and denying her access.

"There are other considerations, Lou."

She looked at me, her eyebrows knitting together in a look of adorable confusion. Then her face cleared and she let out a laugh.

"I've got an IUD, Ian."

I was floored.

"What? Why?"

The moment the words were out of my mouth, I realized how insulting they sounded. I closed my eyes but she just laughed again.

"I had it put in a few years ago when I thought I might actually date at some point. Before I lost hope. Long before you came back."

The thought of sliding into her bare sent a surge of adrenaline through my body. I grabbed her by the waist with both hands and flipped her over until I had her pinned against the bed. I lay on top of her, using my full body weight to keep her still. I reached down between us, grabbed my cock, and guided it in. Not that it needed much help. It was like I was responding to a homing beacon. I was inside Lou Taylor. *Fuck me.*

I pushed up on my elbows and gazed into her eyes.

"What?" she whispered.

I shook my head.

"Nothing. Just want to remember this."

And then I fucked her. I fucked her like we'd been messing around for weeks on end with no release. I fucked her like we were drowning and only we could hold each other afloat. I fucked her like I'd dreamed of fucking her every single night of my life. And she loved it. The sound of Lou screaming my name as she came undone was all I needed to hear for the rest of my fucking days.

CHAPTER TWENTY-ONE

Louisa

When I was finally able to catch my breath and form coherent words, I turned to Ian and stared at him.

"So you're saying we get to do that forever?" I asked him.

He burst out laughing and slapped my thigh, sending a thrill up my leg, straight toward parts way too sensitive to withstand further attention.

"Yes, Lou. We get to do that forever."

"Well, shit."

We were both on our backs, about a foot apart, lying where we'd dropped. Neither of us was able to move. He was still breathing pretty heavily.

"And was that, like, regular sex? Like, the

kind of sex you have all the time?"

He snorted.

"No, Lou. That was not regular sex. That was crazy-ass, mind-blowing sex."

I rolled over onto my stomach and propped myself up on my elbows. I took my time looking him over, from head to toe, letting my eyes lingering on the good parts. Finally, I raised my head and looked him the eye.

"What was your favourite part?" I asked.

"Watching you come undone."

He answered without hesitation, and it sent a rush through my body. I felt my face grow hot as I thought back on how I really had fallen apart, come completely undone under his touch. He laughed.

"Lou, I spent twenty-five years watching you hold it together, watching you keep your cool while everything around you went to shit. To see you unravel like that? Completely lose control? It's the hottest fucking thing I've ever seen in my life."

He rolled over onto this stomach and lay next to me, nudging my shoulder with his.

"I want to see you do that every day."

A slow smile crept across my face as I contemplated the possibilities.

*

A few weeks later, when the warm weather of May started to settle in, we resumed our nightly drinks on the front porch. We'd all pretty much settled into the idea that this virus wasn't going away any time soon and were grateful for each other's company.

I was standing out on my porch one evening, chatting with Allie, who was standing at the foot of my stairs. We hadn't seen or spoken to each other since that last walk when I told her I was falling in love. I still hadn't had time to catch her up when Ian walked out the front door, walked up behind me, and wrapped his arms around my waist. He planted a warm kiss on my neck, breathing in deeply as if I were an intoxicating flower. I looked up at Allie and smiled. She raised her eyebrows, smiling back. She tipped her drink at me and turned to walk away.

"Happy?" Ian murmured against my neck.

I put down my wineglass on and covered his arms with my own, taking hold of his hands and squeezing gently.

"So happy."

I felt him smile against my skin as he continued to nuzzle his way down the back of my neck. I was starting to squirm and squeezed my thighs together in an effort not to dissolve in a puddle at his feet. I sighed, leaned back against him, and watched as Allie retreated down the courtyard path, returning to her house.

My gaze was diverted when she passed by Zach's door. He and Casey were standing there, apparently in some kind of heated argument. I had heard nothing of them since they opted to shack up together a couple of months back. Casey looked pissed. Zach just looked wounded.

"I wonder what's going on there," Ian whispered in my ear.

So do I. I twisted around to look at him.

"Let's go have dinner."

He leaned down, planted a kiss on my lips, took my hand, and led me inside.

*

Want more? Read an excerpt from *Redemption*, the next book in the series:

"You know what I find really irritating?" I asked, peering over my phone at the TV screen. "The way you spend more time browsing shows on Netflix than actually watching them."

Aaron looked over at me and rolled his eyes.

"God. I also hate the way you roll your eyes."

Aaron and I had been screwing around for a few weeks now, and I was rapidly growing tired of him. That was always how it went. Invite them in, let them stick around a while, and then I got bored. Easier to cut them loose sooner than later.

Also, everyone was saying we were just days away from stay-at-home orders, and there was no way I was quarantining with this dude.

Aaron turned off the TV and turned to face me.

"Okay, out with it, Casey. What's going on? You've been at me for days now."

I shrugged.

"I dunno, Aaron. Maybe we're done here?"

He looked at me, slight surprise registering on his face. It was quickly replaced with a shrug of his own.

"Sure. If that's what you want."

I nodded. *Pretty sure, dude.*

Aaron stood up and grabbed his jacket off the nearby chair. He leaned over and picked up his bag of weed, stuffing it in his pocket. *Cheapskate.* Then he looked at me and smiled.

"It was fun, Case. I love that thing you do with your tongue."

I smiled and flicked my tongue out at him,

the platinum stud piercing glinting off the overhead light. He laughed and gave me a quick salute before heading out the door. I threw my feet up on the ottoman and sighed. Oh, well. I leaned over and picked up the joint he'd just finished rolling. At least he'd left that. I sparked up and smoked it while flicking through the Netflix menu.

*

First thing I did when I got up the next morning was call the clinic and book an appointment for tests. Luckily, they were booking the same day. Aaron and I had used protection, but I didn't like to fuck around with this shit. Better to get tested now than get a nasty surprise down the line.

I crawled out of bed and pulled on some clothes. I looked in the mirror, my pixie-cut blond hair poking off in all directions. I rolled my eyes at myself and ran my hands through it, trying to tame it somewhat. Then I just stopped and stared at myself. I was tiny at 27, just over five feet. And I didn't get the tiny body to go with the height, either. I was all curves and my tits were far too big for my frame. Something had to change, though. I needed to mark this split with Aaron like I had with all the others. I didn't want another piercing, and I still hadn't decided on a tattoo. I looked back in the mirror and smiled. My hair.

On the way to the clinic, I stopped in at the drugstore around the corner and checked out the hair dye section until I found exactly what I was looking for—a fiery red. *Perfect.* I brought it up to the cashier, paid, and continued to the clinic.

Hours later, after I'd polished off a few slices of leftover pizza, I got to work dying my hair. I was very careful to protect the sink and counters before starting, despite my messy nature. Thing was, it wasn't really my house. At my own place was one thing, but I was just house-sitting for the year. This Wexler family had bought a new house but hadn't yet sorted out what to do with this one. I had six months left and then I'd have to find somewhere new to crash. It also meant I'd have to get a job. This whole arrangement had been *sweet.* I'd be sad when it ended.

I wrapped my head loosely in a towel and walked into the front room, where I could easily see out into the courtyard. My neighbour, Allie, was just coming home with Loki. I'd met her a couple of months ago when we had this impromptu celebration for her marriage to Matt. The second, and I mean the second, I stepped into her house I knew she and Matt would be the coolest fucking neighbours ever. And they didn't disappoint. Those two got the best weed.

Otherwise, the courtyard was empty. I was just about to turn away when I caught some movement in my peripheral vision. My lips curled up in a smile as I caught Zach leaving the house, trotting down the steps and turning towards the street.

God, he was gorgeous. Like, unearthly gorgeous. Over six feet tall, dark eyes, dark curly hair, a body like a fucking beast. And that ring on his thumb? I'd had many a pleasant thought about what that would feel like grazing against my nipple. That man was fire. Who cared that he was eight years older than me? *Rawr.*

As if he could read my mind, he stopped at the edge of the courtyard and looked back, right at me. I smiled and waved. He gave me a quick wave, no smile, and walked away.

Other books by Sydney Campbell:

Allie Styles Romance Series:
Temptation (Book 1)
Deception (Book 2)
Reckonings (Book 3)
Beginnings (Book 4)

Courtyard Tales of Contemporary Romance
Reawakening
Redemption
Reckless